MW01148111

On Pins and Needles

A Southern Quilting Mystery, Volume 10

Elizabeth Craig

Published by Elizabeth Spann Craig, 2018.

ON PINS AND NEEDLES

First edition. November 27, 2018.

Written by Elizabeth Craig.

To Coleman.

Chapter One

"She wouldn't even come to a guild meeting!"

Meadow Downey's face was indignant as she looked around the table at her friends Beatrice and Wyatt, looking for sympathy. Her husband, Ramsay, was already rolling his eyes. They were seated in Meadow and Ramsay's cozy kitchen for what had become a ritual—Friday breakfast. Their home was a transformed barn and signs of Meadow's passion for quilting hung around them in the form of colorful quilts of different sizes. As usual, Meadow had cooked an enormous spread of food: vegetable omelets, pancakes, biscuits with homemade blackberry jam, and two different types of sausages.

"Meadow," Ramsay said, "not everybody is cut out to be a quilter." He took another fluffy biscuit off a plate in the middle of the table and slathered it with butter.

Meadow said, "Well, it worked for Beatrice!" Her eyes behind their red-framed glasses gazed at Beatrice, pleading for her to back her up. She impatiently smacked a long, gray braid of hair out of her way.

1

Beatrice said, "It worked once I got over the certainty that I was being kidnapped. You forcibly removed me from my house to attend a guild meeting."

"And I wasn't that firm with Annabelle," said Meadow. "She should have no complaints whatsoever. I simply don't understand why she's not wanting to socialize with us all."

Wyatt considered this while he finished a bite of a biscuit. "Perhaps she hasn't really settled into town yet."

Beatrice smiled at her husband. "Trust a minister to have a sympathetic view of the situation."

Meadow said, "But she's been here for five or six months. She should be as settled as anyone can possibly be! How hard is it to settle into this town? All you have to do is find a church, talk to your neighbors, and either volunteer or join an organization of some kind."

Beatrice responded, "But Dappled Hills can take some getting used to. Particularly after having moved to town from a city like Atlanta. The pace is a lot slower. The people are chattier in the store. And people are a little more eager to make friends. That can be off-putting for people who aren't used to it, even if everyone is friendly."

Meadow said, "It would probably help if she had a job here, too."

Beatrice chuckled. "I don't think people like Annabelle get jobs. She doesn't need the income and I'm sure it would seem like a major hassle to her."

Ramsay tilted his balding head curiously at Beatrice. He pushed back from the table a bit to give his prominent stomach more room. "You've been pretty hush-hush about knowing this

Annabelle. I gather though, that you knew each other in Atlanta. What's your impression of her?"

Beatrice deliberately popped a forkful of buttermilk pancakes in her mouth to delay her answer. Ramsay's question had the touch of interrogation about it. But then, he *was* the Dappled Hills police chief. It probably came naturally to him.

After a moment she said, "Annabelle and I did know each other in Atlanta since we were both involved in the art world. I was an art museum curator, and she was a collector. An avid collector, at that."

Meadow snorted impatiently. "But you still haven't answered Ramsay's question. What was she like?"

Beatrice shrugged. "She had excellent taste in art."

Wyatt grinned at her. "How diplomatic of you, Beatrice."

She grinned back at him before sighing. "To be perfectly honest, I didn't much care for her. She could be a difficult person to work with and fairly demanding regarding her personal collection of art. But it's been a couple of years since I've seen her and I wanted to give her another chance."

Wyatt said, "Maybe we should plan a visit. You could bring her a casserole."

Beatrice laughed. "The Annabelle that I knew wouldn't want to eat a casserole. Let alone one of mine." She considered it a second. "Maybe if we brought by some goodies from the farmers' market in a basket or something? She might go for that."

Ramsay was still considering the elusive information on Annabelle Tremont. He said thoughtfully, "So what was it about Annabelle that you didn't like?"

Beatrice said, "She made my job difficult. She was pushy and somewhat of a perfectionist. And she could be condescending, too. We even had words over an ancient sword that had passed into my hands. She wanted it for her collection."

Meadow said, "Well, I'll try again to connect with her. Every time I see her around town, she looks absolutely miserable."

Ramsay finished eating his eggs and then said, holding a finger up, "Now, Meadow. Don't be the self-appointed goodwill ambassador for Dappled Hills. Some folks are *happy* being absolutely miserable. Besides, it's none of our business."

Meadow, who apparently didn't hear a word Ramsay said, brightened. "I know! I'll invite her to go to the Dappled Hills Art in the Park tonight."

Beatrice said, "Isn't that pushing her toward quilting again? The Village Quilters guild just *happens* to have a display there."

"She won't know that—art is art, right? Maybe she can find some local art for her collection. Besides, there will be live music and food. What's not to like?" Meadow pulled her phone out and squinted at her contacts until she pulled Annabelle's number up.

Ramsay snorted and shook his head at Beatrice and Wyatt. "She's already got the woman's name and number in her contacts."

Beatrice and Wyatt's corgi, Noo-noo was sitting quietly at Beatrice's feet. She'd been excited to go to Meadow's, despite Boris being there. Boris was Meadow and Ramsay's massive dog, of indeterminate heritage. He had terrible manners coupled with a tremendous appetite. But Meadow, who was a consummate cook, somehow found the time to bake healthy homemade peanut butter treats. Meadow threw the corgi a couple more treats before dialing Annabelle's number. Noo-noo gobbled down the treats while keeping a close eye on the voracious Boris.

Boris was in high spirits with Noo-noo's visit and currently had a bad case of the wiggles. Boris's wiggles were so joyously robust that they threatened to knock lamps off tabletops. Noo-noo, on the other hand, sat very still in comparison—likely hoping someone would comment on his being a Good Dog and offer another treat in reward.

Annabelle apparently answered the phone and Meadow quickly said, "Annabelle? It's Meadow . . . Meadow Downey. I was thinking that you might enjoy going to the festival tonight, considering how much you enjoy art. There will be plenty of people there to meet, too. And, well, art, of course."

Beatrice's mouth twisted into a smile. The art would be the main attraction for Annabelle.

And apparently, it was. Meadow beamed. "Yes, tonight. I think you'll enjoy it. I'll be there at 6:30 at the quilting booth." There was a pause, during which Meadow frowned. "Yes, but there are many other crafts represented."

Meadow hung up and smiled. "See? That wasn't hard. Sometimes people just need a little push to get out of their shells."

Wyatt said, "Are we sure she was in a shell?"

"That's exactly what I'm saying," said Ramsay. "We should leave the poor woman alone. Maybe she came to Dappled Hills for some much-needed peace and quiet and here we are dragging her out to a festival."

Meadow said, "This is my last try, Ramsay. If this doesn't work, I promise I won't hound Annabelle." She paused. "At least, for a while."

Ramsay said, "And I'll hold you to it."

Meadow said, "After all, people *like* living in Dappled Hills. It's the perfect place. Or it *would* be, except for one small thing," said Meadow, heaving a tremendous sigh that startled the dogs.

Wyatt said with a twinkle in his eye, "I think I can guess this one."

Beatrice said, "No, let me. It would be perfect here in town except for the fact that our darling children no longer live in Dappled Hills."

Meadow said fretfully, "I just want to have them near us again. I'm not asking for much, you understand. I just want my child near us in our golden years."

Ramsay chuckled. "What do you mean, 'near us'? They *are* near us. For heaven's sake, Ash used to live on the opposite end of the country. They live just 25 minutes away. And it only takes *that* long because of stoplights and minor traffic."

Meadow said, "You wouldn't *think* that would end up being that far away, I agree. But the fact is that we don't see as much of them as we would if they were in town all the time."

Beatrice said, "Of course, Piper is still here at the elementary school every weekday."

Meadow shook her head. "It's still not the same. She's there *working*. And then she leaves Dappled Hills to head off to be with Ash in Lenoir. It's not like we suddenly run into her at the grocery store or the quilt shop or the gas station. It's not like we could grab a quick coffee with her."

Ramsay said, "Maybe it's just as well that they have a little distance between us. After all, they're still newlyweds and trying to set up a household and life of their own. The last thing they need is to have us knocking at their door all the time for coffees."

Meadow opened her mouth to dispute this point and Ramsay said, "At any rate, Meadow, you should be able to sneak in a visit tonight at the art festival. Ash told me a few days ago that he and Piper were planning on being there."

Wyatt glanced at his watch. "I hate to wrap this up, but it's about time for me to head out to the church office."

Fortunately, he was already in his work clothes of khaki pants and a dark-navy button down that Beatrice thought contrasted nicely with his silver-streaked hair.

They all stood up and Meadow and Ramsay walked them to the door. Ramsay said to Beatrice, "Hey, what are you reading right now? I've finished my last book and I'm looking for something new."

Beatrice and Wyatt shared a smile. "As a matter of fact, Wyatt and I have a reading challenge for each other. He almost always reads nonfiction and I nearly always read fiction. So we're switching places."

Wyatt said ruefully, "I'm taking a stab at *David Copperfield*. Although I haven't gotten very far."

Ramsay said, "Good pick!"

"It was Beatrice's idea. I have her reading a biography of John Calvin," said Wyatt.

Beatrice hid a grin as Meadow said in horror, "What did she do to deserve *that*?"

Ramsay said, "Beatrice, I believe you got the short end of the stick. If you can't slog through it, I have a perfectly good collection of nonfiction titles in my library for you to peruse. There's a couple of terrific David McCullough books—one on the Wright brothers and one on John Adams. And, since I know you enjoy sleuthing so much, several true crime stories that I know will hold your attention."

"Thanks," said Beatrice. "It's his favorite, so I'm trying. It's just a bit of a tough read, starting out. I'm sure it gets better just a little farther in."

Ramsay looked doubtful as he and Meadow waved goodbye.

As they walked back home, Wyatt held Beatrice's hand. He gave her a sideways look. "If you don't like the Calvin book, you don't have to read it on my behalf. Different strokes for different folks," he said.

"Oh, it's fine, really. And it has the added bonus of helping me fall asleep at night," said Beatrice, teasingly.

He gave her hand a squeeze and laughed. "All right. As long as you know it's not required reading. Fortunately, we're not in school anymore and can choose what we want to read."

They walked in companionable silence for a few moments before Wyatt said, "We wanted to go to the festival tonight too, didn't we?"

"If you're not too tired from the office. Evenings are better there—the daytime events are more geared to children," said Beatrice. "Besides, it's cooler in the evenings."

Wyatt said with a twinkle in his eye, "All I'm doing is finishing up the sermon for Sunday, making some phone calls, and then visiting Mildred in the hospital. I'm in bad shape if that's too tiring."

"Let's go then. We could plan on eating supper there. I'd be happy just having one of June Bug's cakes for supper. She'll have them there tonight," said Beatrice.

June Bug was the owner of a downtown bakery and everything she made—from banana nut muffins to German chocolate cake—was mouth-watering. Before, she'd only baked on the side because she was working as a housekeeper. The town benefitted from the fact that she'd switched over to baking full-time. She also was an amazing quilter with creative and expertly crafted quilts. She hadn't been able to attend as many guild functions, though, considering how busy she'd been.

"Eating at the festival sounds good to me," said Wyatt.

Beatrice let herself into the house as Wyatt waved goodbye and continued walking the short distance to the church.

A short while later, Meadow called.

"Miss Sissy is looking for a ride to the festival and I just can't. If Annabelle is wavering at all on living in Dappled Hills, an introduction to Miss Sissy probably shouldn't come *too* early. I mean, Miss Sissy is *great*, but not everyone understands her," said Meadow. "We wouldn't want to scare Annabelle back to Atlanta."

Miss Sissy was one of the older residents of Dappled Hills and an accomplished quilter. She was also an eccentric with poor people skills and a habit of driving on sidewalks while shaking her fist at any hapless pedestrians nearby. Beatrice would be happy to drive Miss Sissy anywhere, considering the fact that it meant Miss Sissy wouldn't be endangering town residents.

"That's no problem. Wyatt and I will bring her with us. See you there," said Beatrice.

THAT EVENING WAS BLESSEDLY cooler than the afternoon and the heavily humid air was no longer in place. A light breeze was thrown in for good measure as Wyatt and Beatrice picked up Miss Sissy.

Miss Sissy came out clutching her shawl tightly around her as if the temperatures were in the fifties instead of the seventies. She glared at Beatrice and then settled a big grin on Wyatt, who was her favorite town resident.

"Doing well, Miss Sissy?" asked Wyatt politely as he held the car door open for her.

Miss Sissy made a sound that could be taken either for assent or grumbled complaints as she plopped down in the seat.

Beatrice said, remembering past festivals, "Did you remember to bring money for food? June Bug is selling cake there tonight."

Miss Sissy glowered at her. "Got plenty of money."

"All right then," said Beatrice, relieved. Last time, Miss Sissy had wiped her completely out of cash. For a frail-looking woman, Miss Sissy had the appetite of a growing teenage boy.

The art festival was held in a public space with rolling hills and community gardens. The backdrop was a beautiful view of the Blue Ridge Mountains with the sun setting behind them.

There was art on display and art for sale. There was even a potter there with a wheel and lessons for anyone interested.

Wyatt said, "Where do you want to go first?"

Miss Sissy's response to this was to set off with great determination in the direction of June Bug's cake booth.

Chapter Two

B eatrice watched her go with a sigh. "I suppose she'll find us later when she's ready to go home. Or else pester someone else to take her back. Let's see how Meadow and Annabelle are making out."

By this time, it was seven o'clock. Wyatt said, "Maybe we should just look for them around the festival. From what Meadow said, Annabelle isn't much of a fan of quilting. They probably still aren't at the quilting booth by now."

Beatrice said, "You're probably right, but this way I can check to make sure that everything is going well. I know we had volunteers from the guild to man the booth, but I should make sure there weren't any glitches."

But there apparently *had* been a glitch because instead of an absent Meadow, there was a very aggravated Meadow at the booth.

"Never showed up!" she fumed. "Isn't that the height of tackiness? Annabelle told me just as clear as she could be that she'd be here at 6:30 at the booth, and she stood me up." Meadow's face matched her red glasses. Along with her dramatic red and white top and black pants, the entire effect was one of an angry volcano nearing eruption.

Wyatt glanced at his watch. "Maybe she's just running late? It's just a little after seven."

But Beatrice frowned. "Annabelle *did* say she was coming?"

"Clear as day!" said Meadow. "So rude."

Beatrice gave Wyatt an uneasy look. "That's actually kind of odd."

"Odd for her to be running late? Or odd for her to say she was definitely coming?" asked Wyatt.

"No, I can see her wanting to come to a local art exhibit and festival. She was quite a collector of Southern art, although she had a good many other interests, as well. But it's extremely unusual for her to be running late for anything. Annabelle is the kind of person that you can set your clock by. And heaven help you if she's waiting on *you*. I've heard her rant at museum directors and even other wealthy collectors if they were running behind," said Beatrice slowly.

Meadow said, still simmering, "Well, it would suit me just fine if we sent Ramsay over there to do a welfare check. Give her a little jolt by seeing the local police at her door."

"Why don't we just keep an eye out for her and then check on her later if we don't see her?" asked Wyatt reasonably. "After all, she might have gotten held up by Dappled Hills residents. It might just be that she couldn't walk more than a few feet before people came over to introduce themselves."

"I guess you're right. It wouldn't do to overreact," she said, although she was unconvinced.

Meadow said, "By the way, thanks again for bringing Miss Sissy here. I suppose she'll be going from food truck to food truck all night! Don't worry about bringing her back home—I'll do it and find her to let her know. Hopefully she'll be in a good mood after all the fair food. Usually she's less cranky with a full tummy."

"Perfect. How is everything else going here?" asked Beatrice.

Meadow said, "Better than all right! Have you ever seen more beautiful quilts?"

The quilters had done an amazing job. There were quilts of different sizes and shapes. There were quilts with different themes: horses, chickens, and cats. The colors were the best: warm and cool colors, light and dark, and peaceful neutrals.

"They're gorgeous," said Beatrice.

Meadow frowned. "Now I'm just waiting for Annabelle to come over and be totally charmed by them."

Edgenora walked up with her friend Savannah and began talking to Wyatt. Edgenora was another new resident in Dappled Hills, but it occurred to Beatrice that she'd had a much better time getting integrated into the town than Annabelle. For one thing, she joined the Village Quilters, quickly becoming good friends with Savannah, who needed one after her sister married. For another, she was the church secretary at Wyatt's church. Very quickly and despite a rather foreboding presence, she'd gotten to know many people in the town in a short period of time.

One reason Beatrice liked her so much was because she was organized and technical enough to work the church website. Edgenora was able to update the church calendar online and by doing so, prevent the tons of phone calls that Beatrice had been fielding before Edgenora starting working there. Beatrice was, for that reason alone, deeply grateful to Edgenora.

And Wyatt was, too. He appreciated not having a stressed Beatrice at home. He said, "I was just telling Edgenora what a great job she's doing at the church office."

Beatrice said fervently, "Indeed you are, Edgenora. I don't know how to thank you. I now don't have to deal with ten calls a day on my cell phone asking if the church soccer league practice is canceled due to poor weather or not."

Edgenora looked pleased. "It's my pleasure. And now that everything is online, the system practically runs itself."

"You're being exceedingly modest," said Beatrice. "I don't know what we'd do without you." She turned to Savannah as Wyatt and Edgenora chatted about church-related business. As usual, she was wearing a floral dress with a high collar. "How are you doing? How are things with little Smoke?"

Smoke was Savannah's gray cat and her pride and joy. Her eyes lit up. "He's adorable, of course. Let me show you some pictures." She pulled out an old phone and swiped a few times, frowning at the device before handing it over to Beatrice. She saw several pictures with Smoke in a variety of cute poses, sometimes wearing colorful bow ties that Savannah's sister, Georgia, had made for him. He was especially fetching in one picture with his mouth wide open in a yawn, pink tongue sticking out.

"I love that bowtie with the chickens on it," said Beatrice with a smile. "And how is everything else with you?"

Savannah hesitated. "Georgia always tells me that I should look on the bright side. She's excellent at doing it. I'm not quite as good at it."

Beatrice shrugged. "I guess Georgia has a point, but you're among friends. If you have troubles, you should talk about them because it might make you feel better. Believe me, I was the person who *never* shared my problems, but I've completely turned around now. Things are so much better after talking it over."

Savannah considered this, frowning. "What made you change your mind?"

Beatrice said, "I found out that two heads are better than one. What do they call it now? Hivemind? Sometimes my problems can be solved when other people take a shot at them."

Savannah nodded and then said, "Okay. To be honest, it hasn't been too easy lately. Georgia has been super-busy and hasn't been able to spend much time with me. And you know how I was used to doing almost everything with Georgia."

Beatrice said, "I know. And I haven't seen much of her, either. She must be buried in work."

"And I *haven't* been buried in work. The firm where I do my accounting has really cut back on my hours," said Savannah.

Beatrice made a face. "Sorry about that. Do you need to find another job?"

"Maybe. It's more a problem of me just not having anything to *do*," said Savannah.

"Weren't you going to the movies or out for breakfast with Edgenora for a while?" asked Beatrice.

Savannah looked even unhappier. "I was. But now Edgenora is working so many hours at the church that we haven't been able to do as much."

Beatrice bit her lip to keep from smiling. Savannah did sound a little like a bored kid. "Maybe you could find somewhere to volunteer. I know the church is always needing somebody to help out with food pantry drives, retirement home visits, tutoring at the elementary school, or helping with vacation Bible school or youth group. If you wanted to, I'm sure either Edgenora or Wyatt could point you in the right direction."

Savannah considered this for a moment. "That sounds good. Otherwise, I'm just going to quilt all day. That's what I've been doing. But now I'm starting to feel a little burned out on quilting, too."

"Sometimes there can be too much of a good thing," said Beatrice. "By the way, how is your sister doing? I know you said that she was swamped."

Savannah grew serious and glanced around them quickly to make sure no one could overhear them. Wyatt was still talking with Edgenora and Meadow had joined in their conversation. She said, "Honestly, I think Georgia is having a tough time."

Beatrice frowned. "I'm sorry to hear that. What's going on? Is Tony still taking classes at night?"

Savannah shook her head. "He's finished with the classes and is looking for a programming job in Lenoir. There's nothing available for IT workers here in town."

"That's really hard. What about Tony's house? I know they were trying to sell it and it was taking a while," said Beatrice.

"The good news is that he did sell his house so they don't have two payments each month. I've been helping them chart their expenses and budget." Savannah paused, looking pleased at being able to help. Then she knit her brows together. "It's just hard. Georgia is thinking about taking on an extra job. Tony had a lot of school debts and a few others, too. He was hoping to find a better-paying job right away, but it just hasn't come through yet."

Beatrice raised her eyebrows. "But being a teacher is like three jobs at once! I hope things start looking up for them soon."

Wyatt came up and Beatrice asked, "Wyatt, off the top of your head, do you know of any area at the church that could use some volunteers? Savannah was looking to see if she could help out."

Wyatt smiled at her. "We can always use some extra hands there! That's nice of you, Savannah."

Savannah blushed a little and smiled.

"How about the nursery?" asked Wyatt. "If you wanted to go there tomorrow, there's a nursery for several exercise classes. Unless you're going to be exercising, too? I know a lot of the women from the guild are trying the yoga class tomorrow."

Beatrice winced. She'd forgotten that was tomorrow. And she must have been a little crazy to agree to it in the first place. She knew nothing about yoga and wasn't even sure she had the right thing to wear.

Savannah replied eagerly, "No yoga for me. I'll help out in the nursery, then. Is it every Saturday?"

"Every Saturday starting at noon. We'd love to have you help out as often as you'd like. Sometimes it's hard to round up volunteers on the weekend," said Wyatt.

"Perfect!" said Savannah with satisfaction.

Wyatt glanced across the festival grounds and said, "Oh good. Piper and Ash have just arrived and look as if they're heading our way."

Beatrice smiled. This was one way to put Meadow in a better mood. Piper was already grinning and waving. She was wearing a white top with black Capri pants that set off her dark pixie-cut hair. Ash was quite a bit taller and stooped frequently to hear what Piper said over the noise of the festival crowd. He wore a pair of long khaki shorts and a golf shirt. He waved when he spotted them.

Meadow beamed. "They're the best, aren't they?"

"The best," said Beatrice. "No arguments there."

Meadow said with an impatient note in her voice, "At this point, I think I've waited long enough for Annabelle, don't you agree? She has my phone number, after all, and can call me if she still wants to meet up."

Beatrice said, "I don't think you have any obligation to wait around any longer for her. She's running seriously late at this point."

"Good. Besides, I want to finally have the chance to hang out with our precious kids!" Meadow beamed at them.

Piper and Ash walked up, hand in hand. Ash was holding a couple of tote bags in his other hand. They hugged Beatrice and Meadow and then Piper said to Ash, "See this quilt? This is the pattern that I was talking about."

She pointed to a chain quilt with a pattern that looked like a mirror image of itself and had a certain symmetric appeal.

Ash frowned at the pattern as if it had some sort of dire message buried within. "This looks very complicated, Piper."

Savannah's plain features sported a proud smile as she saw Piper and Ash studying her quilt. "It was effortless, actually."

Beatrice hid a grin. She should have known that Savannah made that quilt. Everything she picked to quilt was always highly symmetrical. And everything she crafted was excellent. Savannah had quite an eye for detail.

Ash raised his eyebrows. "It doesn't look easy."

Savannah gave another pleased smile at this. "That's what I was hoping. I wanted it to have the appearance of being more complicated than it actually was. This one only has one style of block."

"Does it use pre-cut strips, too?" asked Piper.

Savannah gave a quick bob of her head.

Piper put her hand on Ash's arm. "See? It's not hard, but it *looks* hard."

Meadow gasped and clasped her hands together. "Is it possible? Piper, have you somehow made Ash interested in quilting? After all these years? It's a miracle! When I think about all those years when I tried to talk to you about my projects and point out little details and you couldn't have cared less!"

Savannah said in a considering fashion, "He must be good at it. At least, talent is in his genes."

Ash raised a hand, grinning at her. "Don't get too excited, Mom. I still don't have a lot of time what with teaching at Harrington. But I was watching Piper quilt and I sort of felt like I was getting the hang of how she was doing it."

Meadow beamed at both of them. "Piper, I don't know how you did it. You brilliant girl!"

Ash said in a cautioning voice, "Now, I'm not joining any guilds or anything, so before you get too wound up, just keep that in mind."

Piper said, "We thought it would be fun to share a hobby. Something *besides* teaching."

Ash said quickly before his mother started getting ideas, "I don't know about doing any of that hand-piecing or appliqueing stuff, but I like the idea of helping to come up with designs and running the sewing machine. Putting it all together."

Meadow grinned. "You make it sound like a piece of dissembled furniture or an unassembled toy or something. Will you be bringing out a screwdriver? Never mind, I'm delighted. Let me show you a few other quilts."

Piper and Beatrice watched as Meadow led Ash off, chatting excitedly and pointing out the finer attributes of various quilts.

Piper said, "Hey, Ash and I picked up a variety of food from the food trucks on the way in. Do you think you and Wyatt and Meadow and Ramsay could join us for an impromptu picnic? It's just that we haven't seen y'all for a while and we wanted a chance to visit."

Beatrice said, "Sure, we'd love that. Meadow had made plans that fell through, so I know she's free. And Ramsay is walking around the festival keeping an eye on things, but I bet he could take a break for a bite to eat."

Meadow walked back up with Ash just as Wyatt joined up with them. "Ash told me and I just texted Ramsay. He's hoping there's a corndog in the bag for him, although I told him that was gross and unhealthy."

Ash grinned. "I remembered his preference and picked up a gross and unhealthy corndog at one of the food trucks."

Beatrice said, "I can see an empty picnic table from here."

They settled down at the table as Ramsay walked up to join them. Beatrice helped Piper hand out napkins and plastic cutlery as Ash distributed an array of food.

"I'm thinking I should avoid the unhealthy options this time," said Wyatt with a sigh and a pat of his stomach. "The fried corndogs did me in last time. No offense, Ramsay."

Beatrice said teasingly, "The corn dogs? I remember it being fried Coke! I didn't even know they could fry a soft drink."

"Oh, I think they can fry anything," said Piper with a laugh.

Wyatt said woefully, "And sadly, I usually think that I can *eat* anything that's fried. But I distinctly remember eating something that later chased me around all night when I was trying to sleep."

Ash said, "Then you sound like the perfect candidate for the açaí bowl that I picked up at the vegetarian truck."

Wyatt winced. "Am I that far gone? I was going to opt for mid-range healthy. Maybe vegetarian pizza. Do açaí bowls really qualify as fair food?"

"No, really! They're supposed to be wonderful, I promise," said Ash. "As a matter of fact, I picked up a couple of them—that's how confident I was."

"I tell you what—how about if I take one and then you can have some and decide if you like it?" said Beatrice.

Once Wyatt had had a bite of Beatrice's 'rainbow bowl' full of açaí puree and granola, kiwi, banana and strawberries, he changed his mind and ate one himself.

Meadow said, "Now that we've sorted the food out, let's get to the best part of the whole meal—finding out how you kids are."

The 'kids' grinned at each other.

Ash said, "This is why I love hanging out with you, Mom. You're the only one who still refers to me as a kid." He looked at Piper. "What have we got going on, Piper?"

Piper said with a smile, "A ton. We're both buried at work, as y'all know."

Meadow held up her hands. "Please! No more talk of teaching. What else is going on?"

Piper said, "Well, Ash and I are looking to move back a little closer to Dappled Hills. Or maybe, *to* Dappled Hills."

Meadow clapped her hands and looked thankfully at the heavens. "My prayers have been answered!"

Wyatt said, "We were just saying this morning that we wished y'all were closer."

Beatrice said slowly, "But you just got settled in with Ash near Harrington college. And you just got the place exactly how you wanted it, you'd told me."

Meadow glared at her. "Hush your mouth, Beatrice! If they want to move closer, let's not try to talk them out of it."

Piper said, "And you're right, Mama. But That's kind of the way it is, though, isn't it, in the early years of marriage? Now that

I know how to decorate, I can apply that knowledge to the next place."

"Are you looking for an apartment around here?" asked Beatrice.

Piper said, "I think we're going to get a house."

Ramsay asked, "Who is your real estate agent?"

"We wanted to use someone locally, so we're with Devlin," said Piper.

Beatrice didn't really know Devlin Wilson, except for the fact that he was the only real estate agent in Dappled Hills. Sometimes people used Realtors from Lenoir and other surrounding towns, but Devlin was the only local choice.

"There isn't a ton of room where we are now, and Ash could use a study. Actually, *I* could use a study, too, considering all the grading I've been doing lately. Maybe we could even use a craft room if both of us are quilting." Piper grinned at her Meadow.

Meadow said, "Which is still the most amazing thing I've heard yet."

Piper said, "We let you think that Ash was just starting out with quilting."

Ash interjected quickly, "Ash *is* just starting out with quilting. Let's lower our expectations."

"But he's got a finished quilt already," said Piper.

Meadow wriggled impatiently. "When do I get to see this masterpiece? And when can I draft you into the Village Quilters?"

Ash grinned at her. "You're completely irrepressible, did you know that?"

"An excellent choice of adjective," said Beatrice.

Piper said, "Actually, I made Ash bring the quilt along with us. I had the feeling that you were going to ask about it, Meadow," she said, eyes twinkling.

"Not in the bag with the fair food!" said Meadow, horrified.

"Calm yourself, Mom. I had a completely separate bag," said Ash.

"Okay, Ash, let's see it," said Ramsay. "Otherwise your mother's blood pressure will shoot through the roof with anticipation." He added, "I'm still amazed you're able to pull this off with everything you have going on, Ash."

Ash grinned at him as he reached into the bag. "Even more going on than you thought." He gently reached into the bag and pulled out a small quilt. It had a cheerful yellow backing and had 3x3 grids of charm squares in delicate pastels. But what leapt out at Beatrice was . . . that it was a baby quilt.

"Piper?" asked Beatrice in a voice that trembled a little.

Meadow had already pounced on both of them, giving them a tremendous hug. Wyatt grinned at them all and Ramsay quickly swiped at his eyes before anyone could notice the moisture there.

Piper said to Beatrice, "We didn't want to say anything until we'd seen the doctor first."

Wyatt asked, "Is this why you're moving back to Dappled Hills?"

Ash said, "Exactly. We knew y'all would want to see more of us . . . and the baby . . . and knew that we might need some extra hands sometimes. Plus, our place just isn't big enough for three."

Ramsay said, "This is such fantastic news. Congratulations to you both!"

Meadow was exclaiming to Ash over the spectacular nature of his quilt and the need for the best baby shower ever, Piper was telling Wyatt and Ramsay about the prospective house that the new real estate agent had found, and Beatrice just sat back in her chair and smiled at the thought of being a grandmother.

They ate fair food and chatted happily together for a while. From time to time, friends would walk over to say hi and someone (usually Meadow) would give the happy news. Piper and Ash had permanent grins on their faces and the grandparents-to-be couldn't have looked prouder. Beatrice realized that the news would spread all over town by the end of the evening.

Ramsay was the first to move. He gave Piper and Ash hugs before saying gruffly, "Sorry, I have to go, but I should make a lap or two around the festival and then make sure there aren't any fender-benders at the parking lot or any other mishaps."

"At least the walkie-talkie has been quiet," said Wyatt, shaking his hand.

"Wasn't that great? Must be a record. Hopefully it will stay quiet for the rest of the night," said Ramsay as he walked away toward the food trucks.

Piper and Ash visited for a while longer and then Piper said, "Mama, I'll call you tomorrow and talk more. We were going to catch up with a couple of friends of ours here for a few minutes."

Ash said to Meadow, "And I'll drop by for a visit tomorrow evening, Mom."

Meadow beamed at him. "Great! I'm making an apple pie tomorrow."

Ash laughed. "Another excellent reason to visit."

After Piper and Ash left, Meadow said, "I'm going to check on the quilting booth."

Beatrice asked dryly, "And make sure that everyone knows the good news?"

"Of course! They'll be so excited," said Meadow.

Wyatt looked at Beatrice, "Just the two of us again. What should we do?"

"Take a stroll and look at the art? I don't want to buy anything, I don't think, but I'd like to see what's out here," said Beatrice. "There's live music here too."

The sprawling fairgrounds offered a gorgeous view of the Blue Ridge Mountains. The sun was going down and the sunset was spectacular with hues of oranges, reds, and purples. The mountains, as per their name, appeared light blue in the foreground. Wyatt and Beatrice walked by booths with exquisite homemade candles, delicate and colorful glasswork, jewelry, and quilts.

They came up to one booth that was full of infant and children's items.

Wyatt said, "I know you said you didn't want to shop, but some of these things look really cute."

Beatrice laughed. "I think I'm still just trying to absorb the happy surprise. But . . . oh, look."

There were; among adorable pillowcase dresses, bibs, baby hats, and knit booties; some homemade stuffed animals.

Wyatt followed her gaze. "The yellow bunny with the long ears?"

"The very one," agreed Beatrice.

The lady working the booth, who was knitting quietly while they shopped, beamed at them and came over to check them out. She lovingly wrapped the bunny in tissue paper and put it in a bag. "Grandbabies?" she asked.

"Before too long," said Beatrice.

The lady nodded. "Enjoy them. I'm never happier than when I'm spending time with mine." She handed them the bag.

Beatrice wound her arm around Wyatt's as they walked away.

They spent a few minutes at the main stage, which had a bluegrass band with excellent local musicians playing the banjo, mandolin, and fiddle. The singer was a young woman with a beautiful voice who sang an especially haunting rendition of "Bringing Mary Home." Beatrice and Wyatt applauded at the end and then headed back in the direction of the food again.

"You know what we need to do now that we've had those really healthy açaí bowls?" asked Wyatt.

"Have a slice of one of June Bug's cakes," said Beatrice immediately. "I'm hoping she'll have her caramel cake there. It's one of my favorites."

Wyatt closed his eyes briefly. "It's wonderful. Except . . . if she has her carrot cake with the cream cheese icing." He opened his eyes again and said sadly, "It's a shame that açaí bowl was so filling. I would eat anything June Bug made. Even pineapple upside-down cake and it's far from my favorite."

"Whatever you can't finish we can take home and have for breakfast," said Beatrice. "And buy an extra slice of both our favorites." She paused. "Do you think we should take a slice or two to Annabelle?"

Wyatt said, "You mean as sort of a spur of the moment gesture? I was thinking that you wanted to bring her an official basket of goodies from the farmers' market."

"I did. But I rather thought we might run by there tonight on the way home."

Wyatt said, "But she lives on the other side of town, doesn't she?"

Beatrice spluttered for a second and then laughed. "You're right, she's not exactly on the way home. And you may think I've lost my mind for wanting to run by and check on her, especially since she and I were hardly the best of friends in Atlanta. But it's just really odd that she's not here after promising Meadow that she would be."

He gave her a light kiss on the lips. "I think a slice or two of cake is a wonderful idea and sure to cure whatever ails her. Checking up to make sure folks are all right is something in my job description, I think. At any rate, I'm pretty good at it."

Beatrice gave his hand a quick squeeze. "Thanks. She'll likely answer the door and be completely annoyed with us for dropping by. But at least I'll sleep well tonight."

June Bug's booth was really more of a tent. Beatrice could tell which one it was from the line coming out of the front. She only hoped that June Bug had brought enough food. She was a funny little woman with a round face and a constantly startled expression. But she was incredibly industrious and modest to a fault. It was the modesty that made Beatrice wonder if June Bug had brought enough cake. Especially if Miss Sissy and her tremendous appetite had already been by.

June Bug was rushing to quickly fill orders. Fortunately, the cakes were pre-sliced and wrapped so the slowest part of the process was taking payments and making change. Even more fortunately, there was no one immediately behind Wyatt and Beatrice so that they could talk for a minute.

June Bug beamed at them both and her niece, Katy, greeted them with a big smile. She was a lovely little girl and coming out of the shyness she'd exhibited since moving in with June Bug. After June Bug's sister had unexpectedly passed away, June Bug had taken Katy in and tried to help her acclimate to the town. After making a first friend in town (a dog), she'd gained confidence to start making friendships with other children.

Katy glanced across the festival grounds. "May I see Jenny?" she asked June Bug, gesturing to another child sitting on a near-by bench with her parents.

June Bug said gently, "Of course! Just stay where I can see you. Oh, and take some cake for them." Her large eyes watched as Katy scampered off.

Wyatt said with trepidation, "Do you have any of your carrot cake? Or your caramel left?" His gaze swept the table in front of him with alarm at the lack of inventory.

June Bug beamed at him and then reached under the table and pulled out two cakes in succession. "I saved them for you," she said shyly.

Beatrice laughed. "Wyatt, we eat so much cake that June Bug has memorized what we like."

"The diet starts Monday," said Wyatt with a grin.

As June Bug carefully cut them large slices of both cakes, Beatrice asked her how things were going.

"Very well," the little woman said brightly. "Katy has all sorts of friends now and she's doing so well at school. Piper has been such a big help."

Beatrice knew that her daughter had helped tutor Katy to get her more on track with the Dappled Hills curriculum after Katy moved in from another state. It was good to hear that it had worked so well.

"But how are things with *you*?" asked Wyatt. "And the shop?"

June Bug beamed at him proudly. "Business is good."

Beatrice said, "I'll say! Your bakery is always bustling and I only hear good things."

June Bug nodded shyly. "And I have some good news, too. I hired someone to help me with all the orders and table busing."

"Oh good," said Wyatt. "I was starting to wonder when you were finding time to actually do any baking!"

June Bug nodded, looking serious. "I was wondering that, too! I used to be able to bake for orders that came in during the day when it was slow in the shop."

"Was it ever slow?" asked Beatrice.

"At first. Sometimes in the afternoons it would slow down. But then it didn't because I started to get customers all day long. So I was baking after we closed," said June Bug.

Beatrice nodded slowly. "I noticed you started closing a little earlier. It makes sense that you were trying to fit the baking in."

June Bug said, "I put up a little 'help wanted' sign in the window, just to see. I got someone right away!" She blinked happily at them. "I didn't ask her to help me tonight, but she's been really good at the shop."

Wyatt smiled at her. "I'm glad you found someone."

Beatrice said, "That would be terrible, feeling as if you were always running behind. Glad it worked out so well."

They considered the food laid out in front of them. Wyatt asked, "Don't we need an extra slice or two? For Annabelle?"

"That sounds good. And maybe an extra slice for us, too. Actually, I was thinking that this fruity cake on the table looked delicious. Maybe we should be experimental, Wyatt," said Beatrice teasingly. Wyatt was totally ingrained in his routines and habits.

"We actually mentioned pineapple upside-down cake on our walk over here, June Bug, but this cake doesn't look exactly as I'd imagined," said Wyatt.

June Bug, taking the extra second while they decided what they wanted to scrub industriously at what appeared to be a microscopic spot on the table, looked concerned. "What *should* it look like?"

"Unappetizing," said Wyatt with a smile. "And this looks mouthwatering. What have you done to make it so delicious?"

June Bug gave a little chuckle. "I used fresh peaches instead of pineapple."

Wyatt asked Beatrice wistfully, "Doesn't that make it almost healthy?"

"Almost," she said, twinkling at him. "All right, let's get a couple of slices of that, too. Then maybe we should head to the car with our haul so we won't be dropping cake behind us like a trail of breadcrumbs."

There was a cough behind them that sounded like the type of throat-clearing you use to get someone's attention.

Posy's husband, Cork, stood there. Posy was a guild member and owner of the Patchwork Cottage quilt shop. Cork owned a wine shop in downtown. "Enjoying the festival?" he asked.

Beatrice grinned at him. "We are. And we thought we'd top off the evening by having some of June Bug's famous cake."

"Listen, I heard you mentioning that Annabelle. Couldn't help but overhear." He paused. "You know, if you want to give cake slices away, Posy and I'll take them. That Annabelle is sort of a mess. I'm not so sure she's deserving of cake, particularly cake as good as June Bug's."

"In what way is she a mess?" asked Beatrice, although privately completely agreeing with him.

Cork shook his bald head. "In the kind of way that really gets under your skin. She's very, very critical. She's the type to not even appreciate or maybe even *like* the cake that you bring over. It could be a complete waste of your time."

Wyatt widened his eyes. "Not like *this* cake? Impossible, surely."

Cork said, making a face, "She didn't approve of a single bottle of wine in my store. Not a single one. She even called my shop provincial." Cork scowled as he spat out the word.

Beatrice sighed. "You know that your shop isn't provincial. And neither are the people of Dappled Hills. You have some excellent wines in the wine shop. The problem is Annabelle. It's just a pity that she's not trying to make friends in town."

Cork gave a crusty laugh. "Well, she's doing a good job at making enemies. Not just me, either. There's plenty of us who she's rubbed the wrong way." He gave Wyatt an apologetic look. "Although far be it for me to tell a pastor what to do. I'm sure your approach is a lot more Christian than mine. Just don't be too sensitive when you're there." He glanced at his watch. "Oops. Posy will be looking for me." He turned to June Bug and quickly ordered some cake as Beatrice and Wyatt walked away.

Wyatt said, "You didn't mention to Cork that you'd known Annabelle in Atlanta." He took a big bite of carrot cake and briefly closed his eyes, savoring the taste.

"I know. I didn't want to put myself in the position of having to defend Annabelle. The truth is that she *is* rude and she *is* critical and she can be quite cutting. But she's also always been a social creature. I find it hard to believe that she's been in this town and lived as a hermit other than venturing out to complain about Cork's selection of wines," said Beatrice slowly. She took a bite of her caramel cake.

"Is her husband here with her?" asked Wyatt.

Beatrice said, "Honestly, I'd be surprised. They seemed to live very separate lives, even in Atlanta. Arnold traveled a lot for work and Annabelle traveled a lot because she wanted to, or to shop for art. But the fact that she's married doesn't mean that she's not romantically involved with someone here in Dappled Hills. Marriage wouldn't stop Annabelle from anything that she wanted to do."

For a few minutes they ate their cake and chatted to a couple of members of Wyatt's congregation that came up to speak with them. Beatrice was becoming more accustomed to this and had grown to know and appreciate many of the church members that she hadn't been acquainted with before they were married.

Once they were both done eating, Wyatt said, "Should we leave? Let's go check on Annabelle."

Beatrice felt her shoulders relax a little with relief. "Yes, let's. Then we can laugh on the way home about how silly I felt when she opened the door and gave me a piece of her mind."

But when Beatrice and Wyatt knocked and rang the doorbell of the imposing house just fifteen minutes later, no one came out to give pieces of their minds. The house itself did not fit into the rest of the neighborhood. The other homes melded into the surrounding scenery and were made of wood or brick or a mixture of both. The outside of this house looked as if Annabelle was trying to be experimental. It boasted an eclectic mishmash of stone, glass, stucco, and wood. It wasn't pretty . . . it was more like a statement. Of what, Beatrice wasn't entirely sure. She couldn't help but wonder what the neighbors thought of it.

Wyatt rang the doorbell again, to no avail.

Beatrice shivered despite the warm night. "I have a bad feeling about this. Although I suppose there's nothing to be concerned about at all—maybe she decided to skip the festival and eat out somewhere. Or maybe she turned in early with a bad headache and is cursing the fact that the doorbell keeps ringing."

"Or maybe there's something wrong," said Wyatt quietly. "Bad feelings should be listened to. We should call Ramsay. He mentioned doing a welfare check, after all."

"No, *Meadow* did. And she was joking. Poor Ramsay is over at the festival trying to work fender-benders in the parking lot. Let's try the door one more time," said Beatrice.

But instead of ringing the bell, Beatrice tentatively tried opening the front door. Sure enough, it opened right up. It was dark inside the massive foyer. She glanced at Wyatt and Wyatt called out, "Annabelle? It's Wyatt and Beatrice Thompson. We've just dropped by to bring you some cake . . . and to check in."

They listened for a few moments, hearing nothing.

"Do you have her number?" asked Wyatt. "We could call her."

Beatrice shook her head. "No. And I'm not getting a good feeling from this." She stepped inside and fumbled on the wall for a light switch. Her fingers found one and suddenly a tremendous chandelier lit up, nearly blinding them after the darkness before.

And there on the floor was the lifeless body of Annabelle Tremont lying on her front, head turned toward them, eyes open and staring blankly at them.

Chapter Three

Wyatt immediately called Ramsay. At first, just looking at Annabelle, Beatrice and Wyatt had assumed that she'd fallen down the massive stone staircase directly behind her. But when Beatrice stepped forward to more closely inspect Annabelle, she'd seen a wound in her back and a ceremonial sword lying on the floor, partially concealed by Annabelle's body.

Ramsay was there in minutes as Beatrice and Wyatt waited. "Murder," he said grimly, staring at Annabelle. "I've already put a call out to the state police, based on what you'd told me on the phone." He shifted uncomfortably and then said, "I have to ask you, Beatrice, what made you decide to come out here tonight?"

Beatrice said with a sigh, "I'm sure the state police will be asking some questions too, and probably not as politely as you are. Of course, I *did* know Annabelle back in Atlanta. I *didn't* like her very much because she made my job as an art curator difficult. I also didn't much like her attitude or the way in which she treated other people. I also knew her enough to understand one key trait of hers: punctuality. With all of her flaws, being late for things wasn't one of them."

Ramsay nodded. "So you were concerned when she didn't meet up with Meadow tonight. Even though we were all thinking that Annabelle was simply being thoughtless and just standing Meadow up. I sort of reckoned that Annabelle was tired of Meadow's pushiness and decided not to show up."

"Right. But being late for an event is just not something Annabelle would do. She was more the type to attend (art is her thing, after all), make a few cursory glances around the booths with her nose in the air, and say something condescending or rude to the various artists and crafters. Not showing up at all without calling Meadow to let her know was not typical of Annabelle," said Beatrice.

Ramsay said, "And you two didn't see or hear anything unusual when you came up to the house?"

Wyatt shook his head and Beatrice said, "I have the feeling that she's been dead for a while. We turned the lights on, ourselves. The house seemed completely dark. Annabelle would hardly have been making her way down that staircase in the pitch black."

Ramsay carefully walked over to Annabelle's body and gently lay a finger on her arm. He nodded. "Not warm."

Wyatt offered, "The door was unlocked, too. We were able to walk right in."

Beatrice said slowly, "Maybe she opened the door to someone she knew."

Ramsay raised his eyebrows, "I thought you and Meadow had established that she didn't know anybody in town."

Beatrice gave a short laugh. "I think it's more that the number of people that Annabelle was acquainted with didn't fit

Meadow's vision of the number it *should* be. Annabelle was picky about whom she allowed in her circles. I don't think her goal in Dappled Hills was to befriend the entire town. But I doubt she didn't entertain here or that she didn't have friends."

Wyatt said, "Then maybe she let someone in and was showing him or her the sword when she turned her back on them and was killed."

Beatrice nodded to a blank place on the wall where metal holders still remained. "Or else someone just took the sword off the wall and killed her with it while she was distracted."

They were startled by a loud rapping on the front door and then a man who stuck his head inside. He was someone Beatrice had never seen before: a gangly, balding man wearing glasses that he absently pushed up his nose. "Hello," he said, suddenly looking uncertain. He caught sight of Annabelle and froze.

Ramsay strode forward. "Look here, Gene, you need to back off. In fact, let's all move out of here carefully and head down the driveway a bit so that forensics can get in here." His phone rang, and he said, "I'll join you out there in a minute."

They left, walking down the long driveway and then stopping. Wyatt said, "Beatrice, do you know Gene?"

Beatrice shook her head. "I don't believe we've met."

The man held out his hand in that absent, automated way. "Gene Fitzsimmons. I'm an architect."

Wyatt added, "And you live close by, don't you?"

Gene nodded. "Right across the street, as a matter of fact. Say, what happened in there? An accident?" The last few words were hopeful.

"I'm afraid not," said Beatrice. "Annabelle was quite clearly murdered." She hesitated and decided not to say anything about the sword. It might be one of those details that Ramsay and the state police decided to keep private.

Gene flushed and looked away. "That's awful."

Somehow, though, Beatrice got the distinct impression that he wasn't exactly torn up about Annabelle's death.

Ramsay quickly walked out the front door and down the driveway to them. His face was grim. "Gene, what brings you over? Seems like everybody wanted to check in with Annabelle Tremont tonight."

Gene shrugged. "I didn't really want to *check in*, so to speak, but I did want to find out what was going on. I saw your police car here, and I thought maybe there'd been a burglary or something."

Ramsay raised his eyebrows. "Is that so?"

"Yes. After all, Annabelle had all that artwork in there. It must have been a very tempting target for thieves," said Gene, shifting uncomfortably on his feet. "I just wanted to know whether I should be more careful about locking my door."

Ramsay looked thoughtful. "You know, I'd probably believe that if we were in Atlanta or Charlotte or somewhere. But in Dappled Hills, I just don't think that we're rife with art thieves around here. I don't believe thieves here would even know what they were looking at, how much it was worth, or how to fence it. Now, if her computers, fancy phones, and car were stolen, I'd think differently. No, somehow this crime seems more personal to me."

Beatrice turned again to look at the tremendous house behind them. Then she turned to look in the direction that Gene had pointed in when mentioning his own house. She said, "Annabelle had this house built before she moved here, didn't she?"

Gene looked unhappy and nodded his head.

Ramsay found his little notepad and pen and jotted down a couple of notes. "Good point. And I believe when the house was constructed, you lost a pretty amazing view of the mountains." He squinted across the narrow street to Gene's house. It was a one-story house with a deck on the roof. "Is that a couple of telescopes I see?"

Gene nodded again.

Wyatt said, "You must enjoy looking at the night sky from here."

Gene said tartly, "Well, I certainly wasn't spying on Annabelle. Caustic know-it-alls aren't exactly my cup of tea. I'm an amateur astronomer. It's a hobby of mine. And yes, before you ask again, I did have my view ruined when that monstrosity of a house was built. I wasn't happy about it. I wish that she'd consulted *me* to advise her as an architect because I could have done a much better job. She could still have had a massive house, but we could have designed it to ramble and not block the view. But I certainly had nothing to do with Annabelle's death, if that's what you're implying. There was no enmity between us whatsoever."

"What have you been doing this evening?" asked Ramsay.

"I've been at home," said Gene.

"Anyone able to verify that?" asked Ramsay.

"Unfortunately, not. As you might remember, I've been somewhat recently divorced. As of eight months ago or so. Divorce isn't good for alibis," said Gene.

"What were you doing at home?" asked Ramsay, still making notes on his notepad.

"I did a little stargazing," said Gene with a shrug. "Nothing I did was very exciting, I'm afraid. I've spent the evening listening to classical music, drinking a glass of wine, working on a crossword, and looking at the sky."

Ramsay glanced up at the sky. "Seems a little cloudy to me for that."

Gene flushed again. "The stars and moon were visible from time to time. Sometimes it's pretty when the clouds are misty around the moon."

Beatrice said, "Did you notice anyone coming or going from Annabelle's house while you were up on the roof?"

"Or earlier than that," said Ramsay. "Considering that it likely wasn't dark at the time."

Gene said slowly, "I didn't see anyone going into Annabelle's house. But then, I wasn't really looking, either."

Ramsay nodded, still making notes. "Do you know of anyone who didn't like Annabelle? Who may have had it in for her?"

Gene snorted. "I think there were plenty of people who didn't like Annabelle. She wasn't exactly a warm person. Anytime that I saw her in town, she seemed to be complaining about things. She didn't like the food selection in the grocery store or the wine selection at the wine store. And, as a neighbor, she wasn't friendly at all. I'd wave and she wouldn't wave in response."

Gene had sounded peeved about the waving. Beatrice understood, though. Dappled Hills was the type of town where everyone waved at everyone else and expected a wave in return. She wondered if Annabelle had realized that not waving made her seem she thought she was superior.

Ramsay pushed, "Was there anyone in *particular*, though? Anyone who talked about her behind her back or who seemed upset that she had moved to town?"

"There was someone who *especially* didn't like her, and that was Trixie Campbell."

Wyatt frowned. "She owns the salon, doesn't she? Nails and hair?"

Beatrice said, "Somehow Trixie doesn't seem like someone who would have run in the same circles as Annabelle."

Gene nodded. "That's true. But she still disliked her. Look, I don't feel like telling tales out of school, but let's just say that Annabelle was a good deal friendlier to Trixie's husband than she was to nearly everyone else in town. I couldn't help but notice the number of times that Elias Campbell was over at Annabelle's house. And I don't think it was to fix plumbing issues, either. He took his private vehicle and not the company truck." He gave them all a pointed look then glanced at his watch. "I wish I could be of more help, but I can't. I should head back home. I wanted to see that comet tonight." He left quickly, loping with a long stride back to his house.

Ramsay sighed. "Gene is sort of odd. I can't say that I'm shocked that he's divorced since he and his wife never seemed to do anything together. He's one of those guys who seems a lot older than his years. Wine, crosswords, classical music, and stargazing? Like I say, odd."

Wyatt said, "But not odd enough to murder Annabelle, I don't think. He comes to church fairly regularly and I can't honestly see him doing something like that. He always seems very patient when he volunteers. He's done a lot with Habitat for Humanity because of his background in architecture. Not the kind of person who would lose his temper and murder a neighbor in cold blood."

Beatrice sighed. "I somehow don't even recognize him from church. And I thought I was doing so well learning the congregation."

Ramsay gave Wyatt a sad look. "You think that because you see the good side of people and part of my job is to understand that they may have a darker side. I wouldn't put it past him, although thanks for a different view of Gene."

Beatrice said, "You wouldn't put it past him because of the fact that he lost his great mountain view, you mean?"

Ramsay nodded. "When the property was sold, Gene made a lot of ruckus about it in town. He complained that the Dappled Hills commissioners were in the pocket of developers. He said that developing the ridge would create environmental problems. He did everything that he could to let officials know that he wasn't pleased about it. And still, the project continued. It's a fine house—a lovely house. But it sure does block his mountain vista." Ramsay paused and then said, "Now Beatrice, I hope you won't take any offence to this."

She gave him a tired smile. "I won't. I'm a suspect."

Ramsay said, "I wouldn't say a *suspect*, no. I can't for the life of me see why you would want to get rid of Annabelle. From what I could tell, you were trying to avoid her for the most part. The state police, of course, might have a different view on things. I know you were at the festival, but do you have a solid alibi for earlier? I'm not sure when the time of death is going to be placed."

"Not unless we can find a way for Noo-noo to give a statement," said Beatrice. "And the state police may think I have more of a motive than you do."

Ramsay looked anxious. "Oh, Beatrice, don't tell me things like that. Meadow will string me up if anything happens to you. Can you imagine how indignant she'll be if she finds out the police might consider you a suspect? She'll give me the silent treatment." He looked thoughtful. "Although sometimes the silent treatment isn't a bad thing."

Wyatt knitted his brows. "How on earth do you figure that the SBI will think you have a motive? I'm with Ramsay—until you became concerned about Annabelle's safety, you were simply trying to stay out of her way."

Beatrice said, "Well, I appreciate the vote of confidence, you two. But the truth is that there's something of a story to that choice of murder weapon. I was meaning to tell you about it before Gene happened over."

Ramsay fumbled for the little notepad again. "What, that sword?" He paused. "And, if you don't mind, please don't say anything about the sword to anyone else. I think the police aren't going to release that detail. And Gene wasn't close enough to see it, so it should be just the three of us that know."

"That's no problem. As far as the sword goes, it's actually a very valuable piece. In fact, I'm hoping it's not damaged as much as poor Annabelle is. It's a fifteenth century medieval War of the Roses sword. It should have 1461 engraved on it," said Beatrice. "Frankly, it should be in a museum."

Ramsay blinked at her. "How did you know all that?"

"I was familiar with it back in Atlanta. Actually, I was *more* than familiar with it. I owned it," said Beatrice.

"What?" asked Ramsay and Wyatt in chorus.

Wyatt continued, looking bemused, "I know you have a nice collection of art, but how on earth would you have ended up with something like that? It sounds as if it would have cost a fortune."

"And would be worth a fortune," mused Ramsay.

Beatrice said, "I was good friends with a lot of people in the art world. My specialty was Southern crafts, but I knew a good deal about everything that passed through the museum on loan—it was my job, after all. A great friend of mine had the sword in his collection and knew how much I admired it. When he passed away, he left the sword to me in his will."

"I don't understand how Annabelle ended up with it," said Ramsay, eyes narrowed as he listened.

"She wanted it," said Beatrice simply. "As soon as word was out that the sword was in my possession, she came to visit me. She wanted the sword for her collection of ancient weapons and armory."

Ramsay said, "And you sold it to her?"

"As a matter of fact, I didn't. I demurred. I had never liked Annabelle and frankly, I didn't want to do business with her in that way," said Beatrice with a shrug.

Wyatt said, "But she still ended up with the sword."

Beatrice said, "My sword went missing some time afterwards."

Ramsay's eyes opened wide. "She stole it?"

Beatrice said, "I doubt that she would do something like that herself, but she likely paid someone to do it. Nothing else in my place was touched. No drawers were opened, nothing was disturbed except for the sword. But it would have been impossible to prove that Annabelle Tremont was responsible, and I didn't think the police would try and get a search warrant on a hunch. I let it go."

"And that's the sword that killed her," said Ramsay. He gave a low whistle and looked concerned.

Beatrice said, "Almost as if Annabelle was still trying to cause trouble for me beyond the grave. And the thing is that she clearly had it on display near the front of her house, too. Showing it off."

Wyatt said, "I suppose she could have just said that she'd found another one and purchased it?"

"Probably. Although she and I would have known better. But that's the kind of person Annabelle was. She was brassy. And she felt completely entitled—if she wanted something, she felt she should be able to have it," said Beatrice. "She wouldn't have tried hiding it from me."

Ramsay asked, "Would her husband have known the sword was yours? Could he have set up the burglary to get it?"

Beatrice quickly shook her head. "That wouldn't be like Arnold Tremont at all. He always wanted Annabelle to get whatever it was that she wanted, but he would have taken the completely legitimate route. He'd have been more likely to send a lawyer over with a contract and an offer that couldn't be refused. No, Arnold wouldn't have known."

"But surely, he'd have noticed the new addition of an ancient sword on his wall?" asked Ramsay, eyebrows raised.

"Annabelle brought in new acquisitions all the time, though. He traveled constantly for work, and he'd have just figured that she'd picked it up while he was away. He wouldn't have thought anything about it," said Beatrice.

Ramsay nodded, but had a look on his face that made Beatrice think that he'd be asking Arnold a few choice questions about the sword later on. "All right. Thanks for the full scoop. Let's let you give an official statement to the state guys when they get here and before you head home." He glanced at them both. "And you even came to the house bearing cake. *June Bug*'s cake. That's a goodwill gesture, if ever I saw one."

The state police were there before long. One officer spoke with Beatrice and another took notes as she explained her past connection with both Annabelle and the murder weapon. She and Wyatt also explained why they were there and what they'd been doing that evening and with whom. They asked her a few more questions relating to the timing of everything and then they took down her phone number and address in case they had further questions. Finally, Beatrice and Wyatt drove back home.

Beatrice said, "I don't know what they'll make of all that. After telling them about it, I even *felt* guilty. I suppose they'll have to confirm with our friends that we were at the festival when we were."

Wyatt said, "I'm sure they won't think a thing of it. They have to treat everyone that way, right? We're just used to Ramsay." He shifted in his seat. "Except they probably won't care that much about us being at the festival. They likely will care more about the time *before* the festival."

"Which is exactly when I have no alibi whatsoever," said Beatrice with a sigh. "And you're right—I'm just used to Ramsay. Ramsay, who mistakenly became a police officer when he should have been a poet, writer, or literature teacher," said Beatrice. She shivered. "I hope I'll be able to sleep tonight."

Wyatt gave her a quick glance before looking back through the windshield. "That must have been very upsetting for you, regardless of your feelings for Annabelle. It was upsetting to me and I didn't even know her."

"It wasn't her time," said Beatrice with a shrug. "And while Annabelle had her faults, she didn't deserve this. No, I want to find out what happened to her and not simply because that will help clear my own name."

Wyatt said quietly, "I know you do. And I know you've been able to figure these things out in the past. But promise me you'll be careful and not take any unnecessary risks."

Beatrice nodded and slid her hand out on the seat for Wyatt to grasp it for a moment.

Wyatt pulled up to the front of the house and they immediately saw two big ears pop up in the picture window, followed by a watchful and then grinning corgi face.

"Poor Noo-noo. She must have thought we'd abandoned her," said Beatrice.

Wyatt said, "Sounds like an excellent reason for her to have a few extra treats."

Chapter Four

As she feared, Beatrice did not sleep well that night. She was unnerved by finding Annabelle. After tossing and turning in the bed for a while, she got up to keep from waking Wyatt. She ate some of June Bug's cake and then found Wyatt's biography on John Calvin and fell asleep within the hour. It was the kind of sleep where you didn't even know it was coming, so she woke up with the sun streaming through the windows, a crick in her neck from her odd position in the armchair, and Noo-noo looking at her with concern.

Beatrice slowly stretched until her body felt like it was somewhat back to normal. Then she got ready for her day and let Noo-noo out while Wyatt stirred and readied for work.

They were just finishing their breakfast of ruby-red grapefruit and biscuits when there was a loud mechanical noise from the direction of the driveway. A minute later, there was a tap on the door.

Beatrice sighed. "That'll be Meadow. I swear there's something wrong with that van of hers. It's making absolutely horrible noises. Is a visit with Meadow all right with you? With any luck, she hasn't brought Boris. It's sort of early in the morning for Noo-noo to have to host another dog."

He grinned. "I'm just surprised that it took her this long to come over."

Meadow did seem to have a habit of popping by, particularly when there had been any type of trouble in Dappled Hills. The good news was that she had become more thoughtful about her dropping-by after Beatrice and Wyatt had married. This was the first time she'd done it this early since the wedding.

Beatrice opened the door and Meadow was indeed standing there, fortunately Boris-free. Her face was flushed as she came in.

"Hi Meadow," said Wyatt politely. "Would you like breakfast?"

Beatrice said, "Ours won't be as elaborate as yours, I'm afraid. But if you like grapefruit and store-bought biscuits, it's pretty good."

Meadow shook her head distractedly. "No, thanks. I'll take some coffee, though."

Beatrice got up to make a second pot and Meadow, who ordinarily would have noticed and stepped in to make it herself, instead plopped down next to Wyatt at the kitchen table.

Wyatt said, "Wish I had time to visit, but I'm running late to the office." He gestured over to the sideboard. "We do have a little of June Bug's cake, if you'd like a slice. And by the way, your van was making some pretty loud noises when you drove up. Maybe it should be looked at."

Meadow nodded absently. Wyatt grabbed his laptop and some papers and books and hurried out the door as Beatrice returned with the coffee and a slice of cake.

Beatrice said, "You're upset about Annabelle."

"Yes!" exploded Meadow. "This is just another example of her incredible thoughtlessness." She took a sip of the coffee and then added several packets of sugar. It looked as if there was going to be a hyper Meadow on Beatrice's hands soon.

"That she would allow herself to be murdered?" asked Beatrice, raising an eyebrow.

"Exactly!" Then Meadow considered this. "Well, that's not really what I meant. I meant that she put herself in the position of being murdered."

"How do you figure that?" asked Beatrice. It was always interesting to get a glimpse inside the inner workings of Meadow's mind.

"Oh, her general unpleasantness. Riling up everyone in town," said Meadow, waving her hands around in a way that indicated that Annabelle's wickedness was expansive and completely without borders.

"Riling up everyone? I must have missed that part," said Beatrice. "Is that what Ramsay told you?"

"That's my own impression. Ramsay was in very late and then didn't say much. But I did pick up the local hearsay this morning when I went out to get coffee. This is my third cup. I got up very early after finding out about Annabelle's death," said Meadow.

A hyper Meadow was imminent, indeed. Beatrice said, "The word was already out? I'll never get over how fast news travels in Dappled Hills. What were people saying?"

"Well, I didn't get a lot of detail, but I gathered a lead or two. Apparently, Annabelle had been quite the crusader on the cell phone tower project," said Meadow.

Beatrice frowned. "I think I remember reading about it in the paper. She was one of the ones who wanted to bring in another tower?"

"On the top of the mountain, yes. Annabelle was, from all accounts, no fan of the cell phone reception here. Her plan was to have another tower and increase reception. The only problem was that the tower would mar, in some opinions, the mountain landscape," said Meadow.

"And people knew that she was a proponent?" asked Beatrice.

"She was quite strident at town hall meetings, from what I gather," said Meadow. "Anyway, that should be something we follow up on. Did you find out anything interesting last night? And how are you holding up? That must have been rough on you and Wyatt."

"We're okay, although it was pretty shocking. The house was totally dark and then we saw Annabelle once I'd found a light switch. I didn't really find out very much, unfortunately. I think I was more focused keeping the investigation off myself," said Beatrice ruefully.

"*What*?" Meadow gaped at her.

"Well, you know. I knew Annabelle in Atlanta and admitted that I wasn't exactly a fan of hers. And happened to mention this directly to the police chief," said Beatrice.

"Yes, but it's *you*. Ramsay knows better than to waste his time suspecting *you*." The indignation in Meadow's voice indicated that if he didn't, Meadow would make sure that he got the message later.

Beatrice sighed. "It's not only that. It's the fact that she and I had a falling out over a piece of art."

"He told me and very sternly told me to keep anything about the weapon hush-hush. I didn't realize that the sword had a connection to you." Meadow's brow furrowed.

Beatrice shrugged. "It wasn't as if I was absolutely livid over it nor as if I tried very hard to find it. It was simply that I had a sentimental connection to it because a friend had given it to me. He was a huge supporter of the museum where I curated . . . both financially and by coming in to shows and exhibits. He was a fascinating person to talk to and he knew that I admired his collection—particularly this ancient sword. I was very touched that he'd remembered me in his will."

"You should get it back, then," said Meadow.

Before Meadow could work herself up into outrage level over the stolen sword, Beatrice said, "I'm not sure I really want it now, under the circumstances. And it could be difficult to establish provenance. I'd have to wrestle with Annabelle's estate. I just don't think it's worth it."

Meadow looked as if she was going to argue the point, but she stopped short. "I can see that. And there wasn't anything else from last night?"

"There was something. Annabelle's neighbor came over. Gene. I didn't know him, but figured that you probably did," said Beatrice.

Meadow took another sip of her coffee and nodded. "Gene Fitzsimmons. He lives right across the street from Annabelle. He's a local architect."

"He came over because he saw Ramsay's car. At least, that was his excuse. I understand that he wasn't really thrilled when Annabelle started having that house built," said Beatrice.

Meadow nodded. "That's one way of putting it. He's a stargazer and general nature-lover. He used to have an amazing view of the Blue Ridge mountains until Annabelle built that huge house. He wasn't happy about it and he let everybody know. Plus, I don't think he was a fan of the house's architecture."

"So that's one person who wasn't happy with Annabelle. I'm guessing he probably also wouldn't have been happy about the cell phone tower that she wanted installed. That wouldn't have been attractive on top of the mountain. Anyway, he was able to come up with another name of someone who was displeased with Annabelle. Maybe he wanted to deflect attention from himself."

"Who was it?" asked Meadow.

"Trixie Campbell," said Beatrice.

Meadow's eyes widened, and she put down her coffee mug. "*Trixie*? What on earth would Trixie have against Annabelle? Did she even know her?"

"I don't know if she knew her or not, but Gene intimated that Annabelle had a relationship with Trixie's husband," said Beatrice.

Meadow's eyes, if possible, opened even wider. "Annabelle and Elias?"

"Why? What's wrong with Elias?" asked Beatrice.

"He's not exactly the sort that Annabelle would be having an affair with," said Meadow. She sloshed coffee on herself in her amazement and absently dabbed at it with a napkin. "There's not an ounce of glamour about him. He does really well for himself, though, as a self-employed plumber. But he's not the sort of tall, dark, handsome guy that I'd imagine someone like Annabelle having an affair with."

"Maybe there simply aren't a lot of choices in Dappled Hills," said Beatrice dryly.

Meadow clucked. "Well, Trixie sure wouldn't be happy about that. And I wouldn't want to be on Trixie's bad side. She seems like the type of person who could have quite a temper. And what's the deal with Annabelle's husband? Didn't you say that they were getting divorced?"

"I have no idea what their status is. I simply *guessed* that they might not be together soon. They led very separate lives in Atlanta and I can't imagine that distance has made it any better," said Beatrice.

Meadow's gaze softened and she said, "Speaking of distance, aren't you just so delighted that the kids are moving here? And with their little bundle of joy. I tell you, I could hardly sleep last night for being excited."

Beatrice said, "Do you think we'll have the most spoiled grandbaby ever?"

Meadow said, "Oh, for sure! But that's because it will be the cutest and most precious baby ever. I just can't wait. And I'm so glad that Devlin Wilson is helping them to pick out just the right house."

"Hopefully there are plenty of places for them to choose from," said Beatrice.

"Right! Okay. Moving back to Annabelle's death. So we have our plan for today."

"Do we?" asked Beatrice. "What about the yoga at the church? We'd originally said we were going to try to make that since Posy and Edgenora had said it was such a good group. Plus, Savannah is supposed to be over there watching the nursery. I thought maybe I could check in with her."

"Next week! We'll start exercising next week," said Meadow emphatically.

Beatrice said ruefully, "That sounds like we're already making excuses."

"No, because I really do want to try it out. The class is supposed to be great. But we have more important things to do today."

Beatrice arched her eyebrows. "Such as?"

"How do your nails look?" demanded Meadow.

Beatrice glanced down to check. Unless they broke, she didn't give her fingernails a second thought. "Like they always do. Neatly trimmed."

"Well, today we're going to get them bedazzled. We'll buy a treat for ourselves. Trixie will do our nails for us," said Meadow.

"She does hair, too, but I don't find getting my hair done relaxing. Too much chit-chat."

As if Meadow didn't engage in chit-chat whatsoever.

Beatrice said, "Manicures as a treat? As a treat for what?"

"You just discovered a body yesterday! And I have just gone through the trauma of hearing that my good friend is a suspect in a murder trial. We most certainly *do* need manicures," said Meadow emphatically. "And that way we have a natural reason to talk to Trixie about Annabelle."

Forty-five minutes later and after having taken Noo-noo on a short walk, Beatrice and Meadow were at the nail salon picking out colors. Meadow chose a grayish blue shade while Beatrice perused the very-light pink section. The salon had old hardwood floors that creaked in protest when walked on. The walls were painted a deep rose and the entire room was extremely well-lit with desk lamps on the manicure tables and bright overhead and wall lighting. Trixie apparently also had a thing for bringing nature inside. There were various houseplants: African violets, spider plants, peace lilies, and a trailing pothos on a bookcase.

Meadow sighed when she saw the polish Beatrice had chosen. "You should try stepping out of your comfort zone. Go a little wild with your color."

Beatrice frowned. "I can't see myself going to church on Sunday as The Minister's Wife wearing *Summer Scandal Scarlet* on my fingertips. Somehow the two things don't mesh."

"At least you could give everyone something to talk about. Just think—you can be the cool grandma! You're such an upstanding citizen that you don't offer anything for the gossips," said Meadow. "Although a past connection with a murder victim might change things up a little bit."

Beatrice's retort was cut off by a smiling woman with very long, red fingernails that Beatrice figured must be Summer Scandal Scarlet. She wore lots of eye makeup, which did little to soften her rather tough appearance. The woman was tall, taller than Beatrice and Beatrice was tall, herself.

"Hi there dumplin'," said the woman in a low drawl. "Good to see ya." She gave Meadow a hug and then put out a hand to Beatrice.

Beatrice delicately shook it, trying not to be stabbed by the nails in the process.

Meadow said, "Trixie, this is Beatrice Coleman."

Trixie said, "Pleasure. What a great name! Makes me think of Peter Rabbit and little mice and whatnot."

Beatrice smiled. "Beatrix Potter. A similar name, though. And I was always a huge fan of her work."

Trixie nodded. "Fun stuff. Y'all picked out your colors?"

Meadow said, "I think so. We're trying to give ourselves a treat today." She beamed at Trixie and Beatrice knew immediately what she was going to say next. "Beatrice and I are going to be co-grandmas! Piper and Ash are expecting."

Trixie grinned at her, revealing a row of perfect white teeth. "Congratulations to y'all! Cool news. And hon, if you wanted to give yourselves a treat, you've picked the right place to do it."

Another nail technician worked on Meadow's hands while Trixie worked on Beatrice's.

Meadow was prattling on about going crib shopping and decorating non-existent nurseries. Then she abruptly seemed to recall the original purpose of their visit to Trixie's salon. "Anyway, that's our wonderful news. But we also have some stressful stuff going on at the same time that isn't nearly as fun to talk about."

"So what is it that y'all so desperately need a break from then? Quilting?" Trixie smiled at Beatrice. "Dumplin' over there will never let me put on acrylics because of her quilting. Says it'll get in the way of her hand-piecing and whatnot. And she's tried to get me to join a guild for *years*."

Beatrice could only imagine.

Meadow chimed in, "We need a treat to distract us from something really awful. The most horrible thing happened last night. I'm sure you've probably already heard about it because they were even talking in the coffee shop this morning. Annabelle Tremont is dead."

There was an undefined glitter in Trixie's eyes. "I did hear about that. But at a salon, you hear everything, practically before it even happens."

"Did Annabelle ever stop in here?" asked Beatrice.

Trixie shrugged. "She came in here once, snooty as you please. Complained about the polish selection, didn't like the colors we carried, and was rude about my nails. Can you believe it?"

Beatrice could certainly believe it. That sounded exactly like Annabelle.

Trixie paused and gave Beatrice and Meadow a considering look before saying, "Look, there's probably talk all over town, right? The way I see it is that it's good for me to put my own story out there to counteract the gossip."

"Your own story?" gaped Meadow.

"That's right. You see, I'm not real happy with Elias right now and I wasn't real happy with Miss Snooty either, truth be told. Those two were having an affair." Trixie said the word as if it caused a bad taste in her mouth. She studied both of them and then gave a harsh laugh. "See what I mean? Neither one of y'all is even surprised at that news. Word gets around. Anyway, here's what happened. I found out about the affair, see."

Meadow and Beatrice nodded. Meadow asked breathlessly, "How did you find out?"

"Because Elias ain't all that bright sometimes. I love him and all, but sometimes he ain't the sharpest tool in the shed, know what I mean? He just couldn't keep up with all the secrets. Plus, he was dumb enough to put Miss Snooty's number and name into his contacts list. She texted him when he was taking the trash out and I saw his phone light up with her name, number, and even a picture."

Meadow gasped. "Were you furious?"

Trixie shrugged. "You know, sometimes when I'm really mad, I just get super-still. I think that scares Elias more than anything. Anyway, I confronted him with it and he confessed right away. Hung his head and looked all pitiful. I gave him an ultimatum."

Beatrice said, "And he stopped the affair?"

Trixie gave a pleased bob of her head. "Sure as shootin'. He knew what side his bread was buttered on. That Annabelle wasn't going to marry him and make him the king of her castle, was she? Better to take the life you know and stick with the one who stuck with you."

Meadow said, "You seem like you have such a good attitude about it all. Weren't you mad?"

"Livid," drawled Trixie. "But I knew that Elias was going to come to his senses, and he did. I blame that woman for it, a hundred percent. He's never done anything like that before and I don't think he ever will again."

"Did you ever approach Annabelle about it?" asked Beatrice as Trixie put a topcoat on her polish. She had to admit that her nails had never looked better. She should have come here to get her nails done before the wedding instead of attempting the job herself.

"Nope," said Trixie, leaning over to focus on the task at hand. "Would have lost my temper, wouldn't I? I didn't like her and didn't want to spend time with her, anyway." She jerked her head up to look at Beatrice and Meadow. "And before any of the town busybodies start flapping their jaws, I had nothing to do with Miss Snooty's death."

"Were you at the festival last night?" asked Meadow.

"Couldn't make it, which is a shame since I absolutely love the fair food. I could eat my weight in those Krispy Kreme Doughnuts dipped in bacon. But I worked late last night and was the one who closed up the shop, so I couldn't make it by. I wouldn't have wanted to go by myself, anyway, and Elias wasn't available. It was too bad that I stayed here late because nobody came in. Guess they were all at the festival." Trixie sat back and surveyed her own work with a critical eye.

Beatrice said, "You've done an amazing job, Trixie."

She grinned at her. "It's not half-bad, is it?"

Meadow wiggled her own brightly colored nails and sighed. "I always feel so much better when I've had my nails done."

"Spread the word," said Trixie with a dry cackle. Beatrice suspected a smoking habit.

Beatrice asked, "Going back to Annabelle's death for a second. Do you have any idea who could have done such a thing? Was anyone upset with Annabelle that you know about? I'm guessing as someone who works in a salon that you hear a lot of town gossip."

Trixie lifted an eyebrow. "Oh, sweetie, I hear it all. Good, bad, and ugly. Can't help it. People seem to pour out their souls to their hairdressers, bartenders, and nail techs. I can tell you that Annabelle had people talking about her all the time. Most folks were just curious. Some thought her big house was tacky and didn't fit into the landscape or Dappled Hills in general."

Meadow nodded. "It did sort of stand out."

"Worse than a sore thumb," said Trixie emphatically. "I've never set foot in the house, but I bet it's just as tacky on the inside as it is on the outside. Then there were those folks who complained that she wasn't sociable at all."

Beatrice said ruefully, "Introverts aren't really tolerated in the small-town setting."

Trixie shrugged. "Depends on the introvert. We've got some quiet people here that like to keep to themselves. And folks just leave them alone, figuring that they're just minding their own business and prefer their own company. But then there are *other* introverts, the kind like Annabelle. She has just a little too much money and status to keep to herself if you know what I mean. Wouldn't have hurt her to go out for brunch with a group of girls, you know. Better than trying to steal other people's husbands, anyway." Her eyes glittered with sarcastic humor.

Beatrice said slowly, "You're saying that when a rich person wants to keep to themselves, other people translate that as being snooty or condescending."

Trixie nodded. "Exactly. Especially when she acts that way in public all the time, anyway." She paused. "There was one person who acted like she disliked Miss Annabelle more than most. Goldie."

Beatrice lifted her eyebrows. "Goldie as in Goldie Parsons, our downtown revitalization person?"

Meadow said, "Surely she couldn't do something like that?" Meadow had a habit of acting completely scandalized at the notion that anyone she knew, or really, anyone in the town of Dappled Hills, could have done something illegal.

Trixie smiled at her. "I know exactly what you mean. Seems like a real girl scout, doesn't she? Butter wouldn't melt in her mouth. But I'm telling you, she was upset something fierce at Annabelle Tremont."

Beatrice said, "Did this have anything to do with the fact that Annabelle wanted to put a cell phone tower up on the top of the mountain?"

Trixie said, "That was one of the reasons. She was also upset that Annabelle was so scornful and condescending of what she's trying to do downtown."

"Wait," said Meadow, sounding outraged, "You're saying that Annabelle somehow found fault with the way that Goldie is trying to make Dappled Hills a better place? The heritage program, the recycling program, the downtown revitalization, the tourism?"

Trixie shrugged again. "She just said that Annabelle called the town a dump. That made her so mad that she had tears coming out of her eyes."

"I should say so!" said Meadow indignantly. "The very idea. The mountain vistas make Dappled Hills a destination and downtown is absolutely charming with the precious shops, great dining and the beautiful old buildings with the exposed brick walls."

Trixie raised her eyebrows. "Sounds like you should be working in Goldie's office, Meadow. But then, you've always been a cheerleader for Dappled Hills."

"What else did Goldie say?" asked Beatrice.

"She was mad that Annabelle had belittled her work and said that Goldie's efforts were useless. And she was mad that Annabelle didn't say it privately but in a public forum—a town hall meeting. Goldie had given this full presentation to the small business owners and local residents with all the things she was working on. Then Annabelle stood up and ranted about how Dappled Hills wasn't going anywhere with her plan. That Dappled Hills needed to focus more on being a resort town that had more high-end amenities and stuff. Spas, fancy restaurants, upscale hotels and houses for rent."

Beatrice said, "Goldie was embarrassed at Annabelle calling her out like that, I'm sure."

"Or furious," said Trixie with a laconic smile as she put Beatrice's nails under the dryer.

Meadow said, "Still, I can't see Goldie Parsons heading over to Annabelle's house and killing her over some hurt feelings."

Trixie snorted. "You didn't see Goldie's face or hear her when she was talking about it."

Chapter Five

When Beatrice and Meadow's nails were dry, they stood to go.

"Before you head out, y'all should try this shampoo. It's on sale this week and it performs miracles on your hair," said Trixie in a practiced but persuasive voice. She held out a large bottle of shampoo. "It will especially help when the seasons change and we start running the heat. Heat can really dry your hair out."

Beatrice demurred, but Meadow asked, "Does it take care of split ends? I'm always having a problem with those." She gestured to her long, gray braid.

Trixie nodded. "You'll be amazed."

"Okay, sure, I'll give it a try."

A few minutes later, they were leaving with the bottle of shampoo in hand. Beatrice was ready to head out before any more sales pitches were made.

"Don't you feel better?" asked Meadow. "There's something about getting your nails done that just helps me to de-stress."

"I feel better except for the fact that there are even more leads now as to who might have murdered Annabelle," said Beatrice.

Meadow rolled her eyes. "Do you really think that Goldie Parsons could have something to do with Annabelle's death? You've seen her—she's as wholesome as they come. Her parents should have named her *Goodie* instead of *Goldie*. Trixie is right—she's a girl scout."

Beatrice said, "I'll admit that I have a hard time picturing it. But then, I have a hard time seeing *anyone* in Dappled Hills as a killer. Gene Fitzsimmons is as mild-mannered as they come. I mean, the guy admitted to spending his evening with a crossword puzzle and classical music. But from all accounts, he was apparently furious over Annabelle blocking his view with her house. And Trixie seems easy-going but I can't imagine she was as laid-back as she seemed over Elias's affair with Annabelle."

Meadow nodded. "I know what you mean. I can't really picture Trixie sitting down and having a calm and businesslike meeting with her husband and quietly giving him an ultimatum. There must have been more to it than that. I don't think Trixie would take kindly to being treated that way."

"So if Gene and Trixie could get that angry, why couldn't Goldie get fired up when Annabelle publicly humiliated her? Maybe having her efforts belittled like that was the final straw and Goldie lost it," said Beatrice.

"And tramped over to Annabelle's house, pulled an ancient ceremonial sword off the wall, and stabbed Annabelle with it?" asked Meadow, shaking her head as if the vision in her mind was completely incompatible with what she knew of Goldie.

"Let's go over and talk with Goldie. We have time, don't we?" asked Beatrice.

Meadow said, "Do we?"

"I don't know, I'm asking you," said Beatrice with a grin. "I've suddenly even managed to forget what day of the week it is and what my schedule looks like."

Meadow said, "Because it's been too busy! It's the weekend, so there probably aren't any plans. Of course, weekends are busy for Wyatt. That's when he really has to get that sermon nailed down before it's delivered on Sunday. But as far as I know, you and I don't have anything going on. Oh, except for the guild meeting on Monday. Posy's hosting it at her shop, remember?"

"Got it," said Beatrice. "So let's see if we can catch up with Goldie. I guess she'll be in the town hall?"

"She's either in the town hall or she's out walking around downtown, visiting small business owners," said Meadow. "Goldie is always working. She's doing her best to make Dappled Hills even better and I can't for the life of me figure out why Annabelle would make her feel badly about her efforts. I love the downtown revitalization she's starting. But let's run by the Patchwork Cottage on the way. I need to pick up a couple of things there for my latest project."

The two women entered the Patchwork Cottage minutes later. Posy was the shop owner and had created a cozy craft haven in the store. Quilts hung everywhere, even over an antique washstand and an old sewing machine. She now had a display case where proud local quilters would hang pictures of their award-winning quilts. Soft music was piped in, usually by a local artist. And today, the cozy atmosphere was enhanced by the smell of brownies. Posy had apparently been cooking and the delicious results were on a small table along with a pitcher of sweet tea.

Posy immediately came over and gave them both a quick hug. As usual, she was wearing a fluffy cardigan sweater (this one was a light blue with a whimsical cat pin on it) and a kind expression. Beatrice had often thought how sweet her friend was and how funny it was that she'd always had such a good relationship with her rather irascible husband, Cork.

"Come have some brownies," she said. "Otherwise, you're dooming me to eating them, myself!"

"I keep forgetting that you have a kitchen here," said Meadow. "We should throw a party here some time. I could cook for us!"

Posy's eyes twinkled. "That sounds delicious except for the fact that it's a miniature kitchen. I'm not sure how much cooking you could do. It's perfect for a batch of brownies, though." She put her hand over her mouth. "Oh! And before I say anything else, I heard your happy news last night! Congratulations to both of you. Just think . . . grandmamas!"

Beatrice said, "It made my day yesterday. Actually, the news is making my day today, too."

Meadow said, "Beatrice is still happily absorbing the info. I'm moving forward into buying baby gear. Maybe we can go in together on a stroller, Beatrice? That's kind of a big-ticket item."

They chatted for a few minutes about baby preparation and Meadow had Posy show her the latest fabrics that she had in for baby quilts and lap blankets. There was an adorable fabric that drew Beatrice in. It featured cute racoons, fawns, foxes, bunnies, and butterflies scattered across a field dotted with red-and-white-spotted mushrooms.

Posy said, "That will make a precious quilt, Beatrice."

"Could I have two yards of it? It's really calling out to me," said Beatrice. "Maybe I'll put my other quilt on hold and finish a baby quilt first."

As Posy checked her out at the cash register, Beatrice had a bite of a brownie. "Mm. These are still warm. At some point, I'm going to be paying for the fact that I've been eating all of this good food lately. Breakfast at Meadow's, June Bug's cake, and now brownies at the quilt shop!" She put a hand lightly on her tummy as if expecting it to puff up from the long litany of delicious food. Then she started, feeling something brush against her leg.

Posy smiled at her. "It's just Maisie," she said.

"I must be a little jumpy still," muttered Beatrice as she reached down to stroke the shop cat.

The door chimed, and they turned around to see Goldie Parsons walk in. Meadow, never one to be subtle, jabbed Beatrice pointedly with her elbow.

Goldie beamed at them, dimples flashing. "It smells like brownies in here!" She had brown hair which she'd pulled up into a ponytail. She had on a rather shapeless skirt and top and shoes designed for comfort instead of style.

Posy said, "Good to see you, Goldie!"

Meadow said with a delighted smile, "Are you taking up quilting?"

Goldie put a hand out as if to ward off an over-zealous Meadow. It was wise to stop her before she went into full-fledged rush mode. Beatrice had been the recipient of her recruitment strategies before.

Goldie said, "I'm afraid not! But I admire them so much," she added quickly as Meadow's face became crestfallen. "No, I'm here today as part of the downtown revitalization project. I was also going to go by Cork's store, but I figured maybe I could knock out two birds with one stone and you could fill him in, Posy?"

Posy smiled at her. "Of course I can. Cork and I have been so pleased with all of your work for Dappled Hills. Your anti-litter campaign worked out so well. I love how the streets are so much cleaner."

Meadow said, "And the campaign is still going strong! Having a group of volunteers to pick up what litter there *is* was a great idea. I never see trash on the sides of the roads anymore."

Goldie looked pleased. "Thanks so much! Now let me tell y'all about the next step in our tourism and revitalization efforts."

For the next five or ten minutes, Goldie ran through a list of objectives for her department and how shop owners could help out. Beatrice and Meadow nibbled on brownies and listened in.

At the end, Posy said warmly, "Well, it all sounds just terrific. Cork and I will be happy to help out, of course. I know that we're going to end up being a tourist destination, especially with the plans that you have."

Meadow said, "I've always said that an apple festival would be a wonderful idea here. Other towns do it and have tons of tourists that come in. We could have bounce-houses, face-painting, and balloon animals for the kids and then music and food trucks for the adults."

"You should try to persuade the orchards to have a 'pick your own apples' day to coincide with the festival," offered Beatrice. "That's always popular in the big cities. They love to come out to small towns and do that sort of thing. It makes everyone feel good, heading off into the country to do something that you can't do in an urban area. I bet a lot of folks from Charlotte would head over."

Goldie carefully made notes in her notebook. "Great idea!"

The bell chimed again and Posy said, "Excuse me," as she hurried off to help a customer.

Meadow gave Beatrice a pointed look and Beatrice said, "These seem like such smart plans for the town. I can't imagine who would ever be against them."

Goldie made a face. "Well, now I feel bad saying anything, but unfortunately not *everybody* has been on board." She paused and then continued in a low voice, "Annabelle Tremont was particularly outspoken about them."

"But *why*? I don't understand what she could possibly have had against them," said Meadow.

Goldie sighed. "I think she believed that Dappled Hills was too sweet and provincial. She wanted the town to be more like Atlanta instead of playing up our cuteness."

Beatrice said, "Surely not. The whole reason that people like Annabelle and me move away from places like Atlanta is to escape the city and find a completely different experience."

Goldie nodded. "Of course. But Annabelle's expectations were apparently not in line with the move. She expected that we would still offer the same amenities that she was able to find in Atlanta. And the same services. She was hoping we could build

Dappled Hills into more of a resort instead of focusing on family-friendly festivals."

Beatrice said, "I understand that she wasn't pleasant about it, either."

"You could say that. She was very condescending when she spoke. Annabelle thought that we were taking completely the wrong approach," said Goldie unhappily. She paused and then added, as if being unable to say something unpleasant about someone, "But I think her heart was in the right place. She wanted Dappled Hills to be more successful. She just had a different vision."

Meadow snorted. "I don't think that she was concerned about Dappled Hills at *all*. I think she simply wanted the convenience of getting the luxuries that she was used to in Atlanta. She wanted to make Dappled Hills upscale." This idea apparently infuriated Meadow, and she flushed an angry red.

Beatrice said, "At any rate, Annabelle and her unpopular opinions are no longer around."

Goldie looked guilty. "Yes. And I feel terrible about the ugly emotions I still have about her. I understand that she was murdered." She winced at the last word. Murder and town improvement usually didn't go hand-in-hand. Then she put her hand on her mouth. "Didn't I hear that you and Wyatt discovered her?"

Beatrice said, "That's right." She shivered and tried not to think of that moment when the lights had come on and she'd seen Annabelle's body.

"Did you find out any more information about what happened?" asked Goldie. "I mean, it just seems so unreal that I can't wrap my head around it. One moment she's alive and well and so . . . vital. The next thing I hear, she's gone. It's just so abrupt."

Beatrice said, "All I can really say is that the house wasn't broken into. She probably knew her attacker."

This was too much for Meadow. Despite realizing that the killer *must* be a town resident and not someone from out of town, she said, "Maybe not! Maybe Annabelle just kept her door unlocked all the time. Maybe some sort of itinerant criminal stopped by and murdered her."

Beatrice raised her eyebrows. "Without stealing anything? Not unless you know something from Ramsay that I don't."

Meadow's shoulders slumped. "No, he mentioned this morning that nothing appeared to be stolen. Annabelle's husband was actually somewhere in Dappled Hills yesterday. He wasn't at the house though, obviously. Ramsay said he'd been fishing or hiking or something."

Beatrice said, "And no one who is used to living in Atlanta keeps their door unlocked. That simply wouldn't be a habit that they'd have."

Goldie said with a frown, "So Annabelle's *husband* is here? Somehow I had the impression that she didn't have a husband."

Probably because Annabelle was having affairs and wasn't careful about keeping them quiet. Beatrice said, "She does. His name is Arnold. I didn't realize that he was in town, however. I think that they probably live apart most of the time. Maybe he came up to visit for the weekend."

Goldie blinked. "That seems like a very strange way to conduct a marriage."

"I guess it worked for them," said Beatrice with a shrug. She paused. "Goldie, do you have any idea who might have done something like this? I know Annabelle wasn't the most popular person in town."

Goldie gave a nervous laugh. "I probably would have thought it was you, Beatrice, if I didn't know you. I'm sorry. It's just that none of us knew Annabelle well here and you appear to have more background with her. At least, from what I've heard in town." She blushed a little. "Sorry. Of course you didn't have anything to do with it. Folks just know that you were acquainted with her in Atlanta and were wondering what your connection was. Aside from you, probably Devlin."

Meadow stared. "Of *course* Beatrice didn't have anything to do with it. She was on her way over to give Annabelle cake, for heaven's sake. And now you're mentioning Devlin? Devlin Wilson?"

"That's right." She said quickly, "Oh dear, it looks as if you didn't know. He was having an affair with Annabelle. Except I didn't realize until just now when you said that she was married that it *was* an affair. I thought it was just a relationship."

Beatrice raised her eyebrows. This was Piper and Ash's real estate agent who was helping them to find a home locally.

Meadow looked stunned. "I didn't know anything about that. Was it something that went on for a while?"

"Oh, I don't think so. I think that Annabelle probably didn't think a thing about it. He was her real estate agent, you know, so maybe it was just something that spontaneously *happened*. Although Devlin seemed like he took it more seriously," said Goldie. "I remember seeing him a couple of months ago and he was *so* happy. He was practically bubbling over with happiness. He told me he was seeing someone new. I didn't know who he was seeing until I saw him out with Annabelle at a restaurant."

Beatrice asked, "How did they seem together?"

"Well, Annabelle was on her phone the whole time and didn't seem really engaged. But Devlin was like a little puppy dog, dying for her attention. Like I mentioned, I didn't know that Annabelle was married and I bet that Devlin didn't, either. He looked like he fell hard," said Goldie.

"And probably with very little encouragement," said Beatrice dryly.

Meadow said in a casual tone, "Were you at the festival last night, Goldie? I ran by the Dappled Hills Revitalization tent and didn't see you. Although the volunteers there were very helpful."

Here Goldie looked concerned. "I was there for a little while to set up the tent, but then I left." She hesitated. "I may as well say it since I've already told Ramsay. I went over to Annabelle's house last night."

Beatrice and Meadow's eyes grew wide. Meadow said, "Really? Why on earth did you do that?" As if Goldie should have known that Annabelle would be murdered and Goldie would become a suspect.

"I wanted to have a civil conversation with Annabelle about her ideas for Dappled Hills. I hated how I wasn't more receptive during the town hall meeting. I guess I was just so taken aback at her approach that I didn't really say anything. That's probably why she became so condescending—because she wasn't being listened to," said Goldie.

Beatrice said, "No, she was condescending because that's who she *was*."

Meadow was gaping at Goldie. "And when you knocked on the door, she didn't come, right? Because she was already . . . gone?"

Goldie shook her head, her ponytail swishing from side-to-side. "On the contrary, she opened the door right up. She was one hundred percent alive when I saw her. And when I left her, she was just as alive," she added quickly in case there was any question of the fact.

Beatrice said, "What was her demeanor? How did she seem?"

Goldie said sadly, "She sort of snarled at me. Apparently, she was in a hurry to get to the festival. But I hoped that she did realize that the town development office was there to listen to her and that we were eager to get lots of ideas from lots of different people."

Meadow gasped and put her hands to her mouth. "In a hurry for the festival? And I was being so snarky because I thought that she'd stood me up. When all the while, she was planning on being there and looking at our quilts with me. Oh, I feel terrible."

Beatrice said, "Goldie, you didn't go back to the festival afterwards? I thought it was the big night for getting publicity out for the revitalization project."

Goldie shook her head again. "That was my original plan. But after speaking with Annabelle, I had the most tremendous headache. I called my volunteers and asked if they could fill in for me. They do a marvelous job and they're full of passion for

Dappled Hills, so I didn't feel bad about having them in charge of the booth and leaflets. I'd gotten up super-early yesterday and hadn't had a lot to eat during the day and I think that's what caused the headache."

Beatrice said, "And Annabelle didn't tell you anything else? And you didn't see or hear anyone there?"

Goldie said in a rueful tone, "I didn't, although there could have been someone hiding behind a tree and I probably wouldn't have noticed. I was focused on trying to use Annabelle as a resource. I wanted to tell her that I was interested in partnering with her for the good of the town and implementing some of her ideas. I had the notion that she might write us a couple of checks in the future to help out. The last thing that I wanted was for her to die."

She glanced at her watch. "I should head on out," she said brightly. "Lots of downtown merchants to visit. You two take care. Bye, Posy!"

After Meadow bought her quilting supplies, they headed back out of the shop. "Where to now?" asked Meadow.

"As unbelievable as it sounds, I feel as if I need something to eat," said Beatrice wryly. "Want to run by the sandwich shop and pick up an early lunch? Apparently the brownie wasn't enough. Or perhaps it's the fact that some days, the more I eat, the more I *want* to eat."

"I'm always up for a meal," Meadow answered promptly.

Chapter Six

They walked to one of Beatrice's favorite lunch places. The shop was small, but they were early enough to be able to grab a table. Beatrice ordered her favorite thing from the menu: a pimento cheese wrap with barbeque sauce, bacon, and spinach. She'd wondered how on earth the combination would taste the first time she'd had it, but it had fast become a favorite. Meadow had a chicken salad sandwich with a side of chips.

Meadow said, "You know what I was thinking about, Beatrice? It's going to be really cool for both of us to be a grandmother. We both are moms of only children, so it's been a while since we really got to baby someone. Won't it be fun? I don't even care if it's a little boy or a little girl."

Beatrice said, "I know. I'm starting to wish I hadn't gotten rid of Piper's old toys. I was just so focused on downsizing before I moved here that I didn't even think about it."

Meadow grinned at her. "Fear not! You're talking to the world's worst packrat. Ramsay kept trying for years to persuade me to have a yard sale, but somehow, I never managed to get around to it. There are toy trucks, games, army men, and blocks galore."

They finished their sandwiches and walked outside. Meadow said, "So, back to the case. I'm assuming that we're going to speak with Devlin now, since Goldie brought up the fact that they were seeing each other?"

Beatrice said, "Probably should. Do you have any ideas about where to catch him? As a real estate agent, I'm guessing he's around and about a lot."

Meadow said, "Well, there's one way to go about it. He has a really distinctive car—an old station wagon. The kind with the wooden panels."

"That seems like an odd choice for a Realtor," said Beatrice slowly.

"You're still thinking like an Atlanta resident," said Meadow with a chuckle. "Out here, Realtors don't shuttle buyers around in fancy cars because it just doesn't matter. There are only a few in town, so your choices are limited. Basically, Devlin can drive whatever he feels like."

Beatrice squinted. "Is that his car there? It fits your description."

The car was indeed an old station wagon with wooden panels. It also was in immaculate condition as if the owner put a lot of care into it.

"That's it!" said Meadow excitedly. "Right outside of Cork's wine shop."

"I wonder if that's indicative of anything," said Beatrice thoughtfully as Meadow parked a few seconds later.

"Maybe a broken heart," said Meadow. "We should tread carefully." She sighed. "It sure sounds as if Annabelle couldn't make up her mind who she wanted to be romantically involved with. You'd think having a husband would keep anyone busy, but Annabelle was also seeing a married man and now we hear, Devlin, too!"

Beatrice hid a smile. She would like to see Meadow tread carefully. Her well-intentioned attempts usually resulted in a stampede instead.

"Besides, Ramsay and I are nearly out of wine," said Meadow.

"During a murder investigation, that sounds like a disaster for Ramsay," said Beatrice.

"Exactly," said Meadow. "It's the perfect excuse."

They walked into the small shop and a bell rang as they entered. They saw Cork, who was talking with another customer and lifted a hand to wave as they entered the store. Devlin was in the section of the shop that sold huge bottles of wine. They were not necessarily the type of wines that a connoisseur would thoughtfully enjoy.

Meadow, naturally, walked right up to him. Beatrice sighed. So much for subtlety. She didn't really know Devlin very well, aside from working with him when purchasing her own cottage when she first moved to town. He was a classically handsome man with blond hair and a nice smile.

Meadow appeared to be deliberately chatting with him in a dizzying array of subjects steered away from crime in general and Annabelle in particular. Devlin was being polite, but appeared to have a hard time keeping up with the ever-changing conversational topics.

Finally, Beatrice broke in. "I haven't seen you in a while, Devlin. How have you been doing?"

Devlin blinked at her in response and then to her horror, broke down in tears.

Meadow gave Beatrice an accusing look as if Beatrice had somehow not followed their plan to tread softly. Cork frowned with concern from across the wine shop as the customer he was speaking with looked startled.

Devlin managed to get control of himself as Beatrice pulled out a packet of tissues from her purse and thrust it at him. He put down his jug of wine and gratefully swabbed his face with several tissues.

"I'm so sorry," he said finally. "You wouldn't have realized what a minefield that question was. It's just that I *haven't* been so good lately and it's hard to face up to that fact." He looked ruefully at the wine as if it had been the primary factor in helping him to avoid facts altogether.

Beatrice asked, "What's been going on?"

He sighed. "Well, business hasn't been great lately." Then he stopped, shaking his head. "I don't even have it in me to pretend that's the whole reason my life has been awful lately. The truth is that I was seeing someone, and she dumped me. What's more, she just turned up murdered."

"Annabelle Tremont," said Meadow, nodding so that Devlin wouldn't launch on an unnecessary story of the murder. "Beatrice actually . . . discovered what had happened."

Devlin's eyes grew wide. "Did you really? Could you tell me then if she suffered at all? The police were no help in giving me details." He paused and gave Meadow an apologetic glance. "Sorry. No offence intended about Ramsay."

"None taken. He's awful about giving me details, too," said Meadow, making a face.

Beatrice said, "I don't think she must have suffered." She certainly wasn't going to tell Devlin otherwise, regardless.

Devlin's face immediately brightened, and he gave Beatrice a grateful look. "Thanks for that. It's just so awful to think that she might have needed me and I wasn't there."

Meadow said with a confused frown, "I must be losing my mind, but I could have sworn that someone said Annabelle was married."

"Separated," said Devlin, quickly. "They were about to start filing for divorce. I wasn't some sort of home-wrecker or anything."

Beatrice asked, "Were you the one who sold Annabelle the property?"

Devlin looked pleased with himself. "Actually, I was. She'd sent me instructions from Atlanta to look for a particular parcel of land—it needed to have a great view, along with other specifications. That's how she and I got to know each other, actually." He gulped down a big breath as if trying to stave off more tears.

Meadow said, "Had you been dating for very long?"

Devlin shook his head. "A couple of months. But then she broke it off with me. Pretty abruptly," he added miserably, looking as though the memory stung.

Beatrice said, "I'm so sorry. That must have been awful. Did she give any sort of reason?"

"She wanted to see someone else," said Devlin bitterly. "It was terrible. But then it was even worse when I realized that she wasn't even leaving me for someone who was actually *available* to date. Annabelle left me for, of all people, Elias Campbell."

Beatrice and Meadow did their best to pretend that this was news to them. Devlin, however, didn't seem to realize they were faking their surprised reactions.

Beatrice said, "I know you really must still care for Annabelle. Just judging from your reaction to her death."

Devlin shook his head automatically. "No, I'm over her. Although I'm having to work very *hard* to be over her. I've taken on this huge landscaping project at the house and I'm doing it all myself just to keep busy. But I'm still really broken up that she's dead. We had a lot of fun together. She was always thinking of things to do. She packed up a huge amount of food one time and we took a hike. We ate right at the top with this magnificent view. She made the best conversation, too. Annabelle had been everywhere and had seen *everything*. She gave me a tour of her house and every piece of art had a story attached."

Beatrice wondered if Annabelle had told the story about how she'd acquired the sword. Now *that* would have been a story.

Devlin continued sadly, "Annabelle seemed so alive that it's hard to believe that she's gone."

Beatrice nodded. "I'm poking around a little to see if I can help Ramsay figure out who could have done something like this. That's why I'm asking so many questions."

Devlin said, "That would be great if you could. Ramsay is wasting a lot of time treating me as a suspect. Nothing against Ramsay," he said again, quickly.

Meadow nodded.

Devlin said, "It's just that he could spend that time looking for the real killer. I wouldn't have hurt a hair on her head. I was working that evening, too, showing someone a property. Besides, I could never do something like that, anyway, to anyone. It's just not in my nature."

Meadow asked, "Did you tell Ramsay that? Why is he still treating you like a suspect if you have an alibi?"

Devlin colored a little but shrugged. "It's just that the property that I was showing was right across the street from Annabelle's, near Gene's. And the client and I met there in separate cars. Apparently, Ramsay thought that that didn't eliminate me as a suspect."

Beatrice asked, "Did you see or hear anything?"

Devlin shook his head immediately. "Not a thing," he said.

Beatrice said, "Then do you have any ideas who might have done something like this?"

Devlin said, "Arnold Tremont could have. Annabelle's husband. Even though they were separated, Annabelle said he still became furious when she saw other men. I was always a little nervous that he might show up at the house when I was there, to tell you the truth."

Beatrice asked, "Did you see him there at all? My understanding was that he was out of town but not too far away."

Devlin said cagily, "How could I have seen him if I was working at the time? Besides, even if I *did* look over there, that property is so full of tall bushes and trees that Arnold could have concealed his car, killed his wife, and then left again to go out of town."

It seemed to be a popular theory for Devlin.

Meadow put her hands on her hips. "I just don't get it. If he agreed to the separation and was planning on them to be divorced, what business is it of his if his soon-to-be-ex-wife ends up seeing someone else?"

Devlin said, "That's exactly what I'm saying. Annabelle said he could be incredibly jealous. She even mentioned that he thought he might try to prevent her from filing for divorce—that maybe he wanted to try to get back together again."

"But Annabelle didn't want to?" asked Beatrice.

"That's right. She was tired of his temper. She was definitely planning on divorcing him. So, as far as I'm concerned, I think Arnold makes the most likely suspect. He had the most to lose," said Devlin.

Meadow beamed at him. "On to a happier subject. I hear that you're helping our two favorite people relocate back to Dappled Hills. Soon to be *three* favorite people."

Devlin gave her a smile in return. "Guilty, as charged. They're a great couple and I'm trying to find a place as special as they are. They're thrilled about the baby and I know both of you are, too."

"As far as houses are concerned, is there much on the market right now?" asked Beatrice. "I have a friend whose new husband had a tough time selling his house."

"You're talking about Tony? But his place was tiny—a one-bedroom. Surely there have to be more options on the market right now," said Meadow, looking alarmed.

Devlin said in a calming tone, "There are plenty of options for two or more bedrooms. Right now, we're just going through all the possibilities. It's a leisurely process because they're not in a huge hurry and because they're so busy."

He glanced at the clock on the wall. "Guess I'd better go ahead and check out. Um, this wine is for later, of course. I still have a house to show."

He walked over to the cash register and Cork checked him out while Meadow looked for a bottle of wine. It was a much smaller specimen than the one that Devlin had left with.

Cork's usually taciturn face broke into a grin as Beatrice and Meadow walked up to the counter.

"Posy shared some exciting news with me this morning," he said. "Sure you don't want to buy champagne?"

"We'll buy loads of it when our darling grandbaby is born, I promise you," said Meadow.

Beatrice said, "How's everything going with you, Cork? I don't even think I had the chance to ask you that yesterday."

"Oh, it's okay. Not complaining. Did I tell you that my bluebird family is back in my birdhouse?" asked Cork as he checked out the wine.

Beatrice said, "That's the same couple from the last year or so? How do you know they're the same ones again?"

Cork nodded. "They have these really distinctively colored eggs, you see. Usually you see blue eggs, but this particular female bird lays white ones. There were also a couple of chickadees that wanted to nest there. Finally, one of the bluebirds stood on top of the house to chase off the chickadees and the other one flew back and forth to build the nest. Nice little couple, and in the past, they've work so hard to feed their little guys when they hatch." He pulled out his old cell phone and pulled up a few pictures.

Beatrice said, "They're beautiful. Although I'm distracted by the pretty birdhouse, too! You made that one, didn't you?"

Meadow said, "Of course he did! Cork can make anything."

Cork chuckled. "Posy thinks so, too. She's got some ideas for something I might make for your little grandbaby. But it's top secret, so I can't say a word."

They admired both the birds and the decorative birdhouse that was modeled after the Dappled Hills public library.

Cork put his phone away and said, "Now what's goin' on with Devlin? He's been drinking up a storm. Usually he's a regular customer of mine, but he's really been stepping it up lately."

Beatrice said, "He was upset to hear about Annabelle's death."

Cork nodded solemnly. "Was he the only one who was?" he asked gruffly.

Meadow said, "It seemed like Annabelle didn't make very many friends in the time she was here. But Devlin was definitely one of them. Did you know about the two of them?"

"Nope," said Cork. "Figured he was dating *somebody* for a while, though. His choice in wine got pretty extravagant for a short period. Then, when they stopped seeing each other, you could tell because he started drinking a lot more." He glanced at Beatrice. "You trying to find out who did it, I guess?"

"You don't seem very surprised," said Beatrice.

"Well, when a person is good at something, they usually try to keep doing it," said Cork with a shrug.

Meadow said, "The only person we haven't talked to yet is Annabelle's husband. They were separated, and he lived in Atlanta."

"Or elsewhere," said Beatrice. "We don't really know where he was based except that it wasn't here. He had lived with his wife in Atlanta when I was there, but he could have moved in the interim. Have you seen him in here at all, Cork? His name is Arnold."

Cork said, "Sure have. He was in here earlier today. He must not have been partial to the wines his wife had purchased here or something because I know there should have been plenty of wine in their house. But he was a lot more pleasant to deal with and didn't say anything negative about the shop or the selection."

Beatrice glanced over at Meadow. "Maybe we should run by and bring Arnold a meal or something."

Meadow beamed at her. "That's the perfect solution. That way we can talk to him for a few minutes and can also do something nice. The way people in Dappled Hills felt about Annabelle, it sounds like he may not be getting too many casseroles and things."

A few minutes later, they were back in Meadow's van. Meadow cranked up the engine which responded by screaming back at her and then making other rattling noises and a high-pitched whine.

Beatrice frowned. "Are we sure that this car is reliable for mountain roads? You need to get that looked at, Meadow. Or at least tell Ramsay about it."

Meadow said, "It's just one of those annoying things that cars do every now and then. Ramsay is going to be totally pulled into this case and won't be home enough to take a look at the van. Or I won't remember to tell him because I'll want updates in the short time we have. Besides, I tried to show him the problem a few days ago and the dumb car wouldn't make the funny noise! Ramsay thought it was all in my head!" said Meadow.

Beatrice said dryly, "Well, that's what cars do. They won't make the funny noise on demand. And I could be a witness that the van really does have some sort of a problem."

"I'll take care of it soon," Meadow said breezily. "So, moving on. Here's the next question. What kind of food does someone like Arnold Tremont want? Is he going to be happy with a Southern casserole? Because that restaurant downtown has a refrigerator full of casseroles they'll sell. Ramsay and I are partial to their King Ranch Chicken Casserole. Or would Arnold prefer us to pick up something like fried chicken?"

Beatrice said, "I think he'll be polite and graciously accept anything that we bring over. But fried chicken and some sides sound perfect since I know he loves his fried food. Anyway, it's tougher cooking for one. Best for us to just pick up a single-serving of a fried chicken dinner. It might be harder for him to eat an entire casserole by himself, no matter how good it is."

After they'd picked up the chicken, Meadow asked, "So how well did you know Arnold Tremont?"

Beatrice said, "I knew him fairly well. As I'd mentioned before, he spent a lot of time away from home, traveling for his work. I have a feeling that the marriage must have always been a bit strained, considering how often they were apart. But he's a much easier person to deal with than Annabelle. He seemed kind, and he had a nice sense of humor. He also had a good way of handling Annabelle and her more difficult moods. I was always sorry when I didn't see him with her at the museum."

Meadow said caustically, "If I were you, I would still be so very annoyed that Annabelle swiped my sword. Who does things like that?"

Beatrice said, "That's just the kind of person Annabelle was. I'm not going to say that she didn't want the sword. She did have an amazing collection of British artifacts. But the fact is that I think she was more miffed at the fact that she couldn't *buy* the sword from me. When she wanted something, she expected to get it. She probably didn't sleep at night until she'd acquired that sword for herself."

"I tell you what that is," said Meadow, wagging a finger in the air. "That's bad karma. And look what happened!"

"Well, I think that what happened had more to do with whomever she'd infuriated than anything else," said Beatrice. "But I'll agree that her misbehavior, in general, didn't help and didn't exactly endear her to people."

"Obviously, the sword must have been hanging there on the wall in plain view," said Meadow, fuming. "Otherwise, how would the killer have been able to so easily snag it and murder Annabelle with it?"

"You're right. She had it hanging right there in the entrance hall for the world to see. But in her mind, she probably thought she didn't really even do anything wrong. The way people like Annabelle Tremont think, the sword *belonged* with her and certainly not with an art museum curator. It belonged in a collection," said Beatrice thoughtfully.

"And to think I wanted to bring her into a quilting guild!" Meadow snorted. "Do you think you'd have said anything to her? I mean, if you and Wyatt had knocked on the door with the cake and Annabelle had actually answered? You'd have seen the sword on the wall. Would you have said anything?"

Beatrice gave a half grin. "I'm sure I would have. I probably would have said 'nice sword,' just to see what she'd say in return. But aside from the sentimental value I placed on it because of the patron who'd given the sword to me, I really wasn't dying to get it back, Meadow."

Meadow pulled back up in front of the massive house. They walked to the front door and Beatrice rang the doorbell. There was some excited barking inside and then, a minute later, Arnold Tremont opened the door, standing next to a black Labrador who grinned at them. He was an attractive man with good posture and wearing a pair of reading glasses, which he took off as he surveyed them and the food they held. Then he looked closer at Beatrice and said startled, "Beatrice Coleman! I didn't know you were in town."

Chapter Seven

B eatrice smiled at him. "I've been here for a little while now. I retired from the museum you know."

Arnold said, "Yes, but I somehow thought you were in Atlanta still." He sighed. "Annabelle didn't tell me you were in Dappled Hills." His expression indicated that that was no big surprise.

"And this is my friend, Meadow Downey," said Beatrice.

Meadow smiled kindly at him and held up the bag of fried chicken and sides. "We've brought supper for you."

The black Lab sniffed the air carefully and then grinned again.

He abruptly pushed the door all the way open and hurriedly said, "I don't know where my manners are. Do please come inside. And thanks so much for supper. It smells absolutely heavenly."

The dog appeared to have excellent manners or training or both. He politely bumped Beatrice's hand to be petted, but didn't jump or do a lot of sniffing around.

Beatrice shivered as she entered the huge entrance hall of the mansion again, remembering the sight of Annabelle sprawled on the floor. She was relieved when Arnold gestured to them to continue through to the comfortably appointed living room. She sat down in a leather chair while Meadow said, "If you just point me in the right direction, Arnold, I'll put this away for you so that it will stay good."

Arnold made as if to lead the way, but when Meadow waved him off, he pointed in the general direction. Although, because the home was so tremendous and the kitchen not centrally located, it seemed quite convoluted. Fortunately, Meadow was able to find her way there and back without having to resort to breadcrumbs.

Beatrice took note of a lovely brass sculpture, the exquisite glasswork, primitive vases, and walls full of art from various periods and styles.

Arnold noticed her appraisal of the art and gave a gentle laugh. "Once a curator, always a curator, right?"

Beatrice smiled back at him. "I suppose I can't help it. You have an amazing and eclectic collection."

Arnold gave her a rueful look. "I might be responsible for the 'eclectic' part of that. I was always very impulsive and would buy on a whim. I suppose you remember that."

Beatrice said, "I remember that you always followed your gut, and that you knew when you liked something."

Arnold nodded, looking sad. "Yes. And Annabelle did all the research and tried to follow particular themes in her collecting. We made a good team, I thought. In more ways than one."

Meadow returned to them, also complimenting Arnold on the house and the art. He made sure they were seated comfortably and then sat down carelessly on what appeared to be an antique settee. The black Labrador plopped down in front of him and laid his head on Arnold's foot. Arnold mused, "Downey. Wasn't that the name of the police chief here?"

Meadow said, "He's my husband, Ramsay."

Arnold said, "A nice man. He seemed very kind and concerned. I hope he's able to find out who did this. It's the most horrible thing and quite ironic when you consider it. Annabelle leaves the big, dangerous city to move to the quiet, safe village, only to be met with violence."

Meadow glowered. "It's an abomination! But I can promise you that her death is a true anomaly. This kind of thing really just doesn't happen in Dappled Hills."

Beatrice suppressed a wry smile. Meadow was the town's most ardent defender. The truth was, however distasteful, that bad things *did* happen in Dappled Hills, as much as Meadow would like the town to be immune.

Meadow added, "Beatrice here actually discovered Annabelle."

Arnold's eyes widened behind his glasses. "That must have been awful for you. I didn't realize that."

Beatrice said, "I'd run by to check on her and make sure everything was all right."

Arnold frowned as if possibly remembering that Beatrice and his wife hadn't been the closest of friends when they'd both lived in Atlanta. "Did you?" he asked in a confused voice. "Why? Did you somehow get the sense that something was wrong?"

Beatrice said, "I didn't believe that anything was nearly as wrong as it was. I'd just worried that maybe Annabelle had fallen ill somehow and needed someone to check in on her. You see, she'd made plans to meet up with Meadow at an arts festival that night. Meadow was planning on showing her around and introducing her to some folks. And Annabelle was quite late."

Arnold nodded at once in complete understanding. "She was never late. Punctual to the second. I'd frequently said that I could set a watch by her. Good for you for checking on her."

Beatrice noticed for the first time that there were boxes against the walls and that some shelves were bare. Arnold saw the direction of her gaze and said sadly, "It's going to take a while to get everything out of here. And I'd only just gotten the impression from Annabelle that she was happy with the placement of all of her art. It took her a while to get everything just right."

Beatrice nodded. "With all the artwork here, there's going to be some tedious packing, for sure. I can recommend a service to help you if you'd like."

Arnold said, "I appreciate that. But the police aren't letting me leave town at this point and I don't really have anything to do. I ordered a ton of specialty packing equipment to be shipped here and am starting the process myself." He gazed sadly around the room. "Every piece of art here has a story, so it's as if I'm reacquainting myself with our lives together as I go. Many of them we purchased together."

Meadow put her hand to her chest as if his words pierced her heart. "That's so sad! And I'm sorry about Ramsay not allowing you to leave."

Arnold shook his head. "He's just doing his job. I would imagine that spouses would certainly be the most suspect in cases such as this." He hesitated. "You probably weren't aware of this, Beatrice, but Annabelle was pursuing filing for divorce."

"I'm so sorry," said Beatrice. And she was . . . for Arnold. She remembered now, seeing Arnold, how comfortable he'd been with his wife on the occasions that she's seen them together. It was true that they spent a lot of time apart, but when they were together, Arnold had always seemed so proud of her. He'd always laughed at what passed for Annabelle's sense of humor. And he'd wanted to be near her, which was more than Beatrice had been able to say.

Arnold raised a hand as if to brush away her sympathy. "It's all right. I simply hadn't been ready to accept that our relationship was over. We'd been separated for some time and had lived somewhat separate lives even before that. I think you must remember, Beatrice, how much time we spent apart as a couple. But I wasn't yet willing to call the marriage a failure." He sighed. "Annabelle could be a challenging woman sometimes, but I still couldn't help loving her. We simply couldn't live together very well."

"Were you in town? When Annabelle passed away?" asked Beatrice gently.

"I was *not* at the house, unfortunately. I can't help but blame myself for that. Maybe, if I'd been in the house, this never would have happened." He paused. "That's to say, I *was* in town, but I wasn't home. I'd gone out in town and then on the trails with Barney. We were out all afternoon and didn't come home until after dark."

Meadow's brow wrinkled. "Barney?"

"Sorry—my dog."

Barney lifted his head from Arnold's foot and grinned at Beatrice and Meadow again before laying his head back down again.

Arnold continued, "I was trying to get my head straight when I went for the walk. Annabelle had been in quite a fierce mood before I left and I was hoping she'd have some time to cool down and I'd think of the right things to say to convince her that a divorce was a bad idea. She seemed as if she were quite sold on the idea and that nothing I could do or say would make her change her mind. The last thing I wanted to do was explode, so I put Barney on his leash and headed out the door."

Barney lifted his head again at the word *leash*, but then put it back down in disappointment when Arnold didn't make any move to rise from the antique settee.

A thought popped into Beatrice's head. What if Devlin had seen Arnold? It wasn't outside the realm of possibility after all—the house he'd been showing was right across the street from Annabelle's house. Perhaps Devlin was prevaricating because he'd said that he was too absorbed in the showing to notice anything on the street and didn't want to mention the fact that he'd seen Arnold. It was worth a try.

Beatrice gave Arnold an apologetic look and said, "You must know how things are in a small Southern town. Everyone knows everybody else's business. Someone mentioned to me that they'd seen you at the house close to the time of the murder."

Arnold stared at her and then gave a deep sigh. He stood up and walked over to a sideboard, pouring himself a drink. He turned to ask, "Would either of you like a drink?" They shook their heads. "That real estate agent has been talking, I suppose. I'd noticed him as I was leaving. I'd only come back to get some dog treats for Barney. I'd run out and it's good to have treats when we're on a walk or else he might spend fifteen minutes or more sniffing at something on the side of the trail."

"Was that near the time of the murder?" asked Meadow, eyes huge.

"I haven't had precise information about when Annabelle's death actually *occurred*," said Arnold in a frustrated voice. He took a long sip of his drink. "At any rate, when I ran in the house for the treats, Annabelle was still alive. I could hear her talking on the phone at the back of the house. I grabbed the treats and left since I wasn't wanting to talk with her yet until things had cooled off." He looked broodingly at his drink. "And now I'm too late to make things right with her."

Beatrice said, "Do you have any idea who might have done something like this? I know you didn't live here and didn't personally know anyone, but was there someone that Annabelle particularly mentioned? Anyone that she told you about that she was having a problem with?"

Arnold sighed. "Annabelle and I weren't really talking much in the last couple of months. Although she was happy to pass along the names of the men she was seeing, just to hurt me."

Beatrice and Meadow exchanged glances and Arnold added, "I know that sounds rather shocking. You'd think that she would be trying to *conceal* affairs from me, even though we were separated. But I still knew that what she'd found with anyone here wasn't going to have the history of what we had. Nor the emotion. I was going to remind her of that, but then I lost my chance."

Beatrice said in an apologetic tone, "Sorry again to pass on some local gossip, but someone told us that Annabelle said that she was ending her marriage with you because of your temper and the fact that you were angry about the men she was seeing."

Arnold snorted. "Categorically untrue. First off, Annabelle was the one with the temper in our relationship. Secondly, I've always put up with her infidelities since they never lasted long. The affairs may have hurt me, but they didn't make me angry."

Beatrice said cautiously, "Did Annabelle mention anyone specifically that she was seeing? Could it be that one of those men might have been responsible for her death?"

Arnold said with a shrug, "Possibly. There was the married man, for one. Although I can't imagine why he'd have wanted to murder Annabelle. He was committed to his marriage and told Annabelle it was over."

"He ended the relationship?" asked Beatrice.

"That's right. His wife was making a fuss, apparently, according to Annabelle. She seemed pretty annoyed about it, probably because it wasn't *Annabelle's* idea to end the relationship. I'd asked her what the status was with her relationships when I got here. So there was no motive for *him* to have done something like that," said Arnold.

Meadow said, "But there was someone else?"

Arnold nodded. "That's right. The funny thing is that it ended before the one with the married man. We've actually just been talking about him. Devlin is his name, I think? The guy who was showing the house across the street. He also helped

Annabelle with the acquisition of this property, which was how they met. He apparently fell hard for Annabelle."

"But she ended it?" asked Beatrice.

"She did, but Devlin apparently didn't get the message. He continued trying to get her back." Arnold gave a harsh laugh. "Poor guy. He sounds a lot like me, doesn't he? I have all the sympathy in the world for him."

"And you think Devlin could have done it?" asked Meadow.

Arnold shrugged. "I didn't say that. Of course, he *could* have done. He was there, wasn't he? If he saw me when I was running in for the dog treats, he was there, too, close by. He'd have known that I'd just left and that no one was at home."

"That would have been sort of risky though, surely. He had no idea of knowing when you'd be back," said Beatrice. "You could have run out for only ten minutes or so."

"Yes, but maybe he thought he had no choice in the matter. After all, I'd come to town to try to convince my wife to give our marriage a second chance. For all he knew, this was his one opportunity to convince Annabelle to continue with the divorce proceedings and to resume their relationship. Maybe he tried and failed to persuade her. Or maybe Annabelle belittled him. She was good at belittling," said Arnold with that harsh laugh again.

"Maybe he became frustrated with her or with their conversation," said Beatrice thoughtfully.

"And then he acted out in that frustration," said Arnold with a nod of his head.

They were quiet for a few moments. Beatrice asked, "Did you get the impression at all that Devlin was very focused on his showing? Or that he was on his way out of there when you saw him?"

"Not at all. The very fact that he noticed me shows that he wasn't that focused. He even lifted a hand to wave to me when I'd spotted him. It sure didn't appear to me that he'd any intention of leaving anytime soon. His client had already left the house in his own car and Devlin was sitting on the stairs of the home, looking at something on his phone," said Arnold.

They again absorbed this for a few moments. Then Meadow, breaking the silence, asked, "It's really too bad that you're getting ready to move. The house is gorgeous and has such an amazing mountain view. Are you sure you can't be persuaded to give Dappled Hills a chance? It could be your retreat when things get too crazy in the city."

Trust Meadow to be the goodwill ambassador for the town, even under the circumstances.

He smiled at her. "Despite the beauty of the town and the mountains, I'm more of a city person. I have a home in Atlanta and a home in Florida and I'm planning on keeping those as my home bases. Once I pack everything up here, I'll have it all trucked to one or both of those places." He gave Beatrice a thoughtful look. "I'm a little surprised that you ended up here. You seemed to always enjoy life in Atlanta."

"It was time for me to retire and live a quieter life. Leaving the traffic behind was a huge stress-reducer. It's hard to find a time of day when driving in Atlanta is a straightforward process. There were other reasons for my settling here, too. You may not realize it, but my daughter lives here," said Beatrice. "She's actually married to Meadow's son."

Meadow, always ready to brag about Ash, said, "They're an adorable couple. And about to deliver us a grandbaby!"

"Congratulations," said Arnold, smiling at her.

Beatrice continued, "And in the process of staying in Dappled Hills to be near Piper, I fell in love with the town . . . and a local minister."

Arnold gave her a pleased smile and Meadow interjected, "And they *also* make an adorable couple."

Arnold asked her a few questions about Wyatt and their life together and then said, "Do you think you could give me Wyatt's phone number? I'd like to speak with him about a service."

Beatrice said, "Of course, I can. But I have to admit that I'm a little surprised. You're not planning on moving Annabelle back to Atlanta? That's where she spent the majority of her life."

Arnold shrugged. "She honestly didn't have a lot of roots there, or really anywhere. She didn't get close to many people. I'll certainly have a memorial service in Atlanta for Annabelle, but I can't think that she would have wanted to be buried there. I know that Annabelle liked complaining and was fond of finding fault with places, but she felt connected to Dappled Hills. I was happy knowing that she'd found a town where she felt relaxed and at peace."

Beatrice said, "I'll be sure to tell Wyatt to expect your call. I'm sure he'd be honored to officiate the service."

Arnold nodded. Then he said curiously, "Forgive me, but I remember something of a bone of contention between you and Annabelle. Wasn't there a work of art or something?"

Beatrice said wryly, "You have quite a good memory. That's right—I was willed a work of art by a friend in the art world."

She was careful not to mention what it was. Meadow gave her a sideways glance.

Arnold raised his eyebrows. "And Annabelle wanted it?"

"That's right. She admired it and wanted the piece for her own collection," said Beatrice.

Arnold gave her an admiring look. "And still you retained it. I'm impressed. When Annabelle wanted something, she always got it."

Beatrice smiled at him in return. The last thing she could say is that Annabelle *had* gotten it and that it had been the weapon that ended her life. At this point, Beatrice didn't care if she never saw the sword again.

Beatrice and Meadow left Arnold as he slowly and carefully continued packing up works of art.

They got into Meadow's van, which immediately made protesting noises. Meadow, sounding distracted, asked, "Where to next?"

Beatrice said, "I think that's enough for today. I should get back home to Noo-noo who probably wants to go out for a walk. And I should probably start thinking about what to make for supper or else Wyatt and I will be eating cereal again."

Meadow grunted in response, still deep in thought. After a few moments, she asked, "What do you make of all this? It seems as though there are quite a few people who could potentially have murdered Annabelle. Why couldn't she have simply gotten along with people here?"

Beatrice sighed. "Well, it's never really cut-and-dried, is it? There's usually a motley assortment of suspects and this time is no different. Gene, the allegedly gentle architect, still strikes me as someone who had good reason to be unhappy with Annabelle."

Meadow nodded. "You're right. He's the kind of guy who follows a strict routine every day. I bet he'd come home from the office every single night and go up on his roof to watch the stars and have a glass of wine while he surveyed his gorgeous view. When he *had* a gorgeous view."

"Then he had to deal with construction noises until the house was constructed. When the house was finally completed, he found that his gorgeous view was now completely blocked. The next thing he knows, his new neighbor is lobbying for a new cell phone tower to be built that will create another blight on the mountain. Gene had a lot to be unhappy about," said Beatrice.

Meadow said, "Then there's Trixie. Or Trixie and Elias?"

Beatrice said, "I would ordinarily think of Elias as a suspect since he was having an affair with Annabelle. But I can't see why on earth he'd kill her. He was the one who broke it off with her after all. Trixie had given him that ultimatum, and he chose his wife over Annabelle. It seems to me that if anyone had reason to be furious, it would be *Annabelle* over being dumped. And it sounded from what Arnold said that she wasn't amused about it. It makes me wonder if Annabelle tried to get Elias back, just so she could end the relationship on her own terms."

Meadow held her hand out to survey her nails, causing Beatrice to clutch the door until her hand was safely back on the steering wheel. "That makes sense. And I bet Trixie wouldn't have taken kindly to having Annabelle chase Elias. So maybe Trixie makes a good suspect, then."

"She *was* a woman scorned. Trixie might have held a grudge. Although it sounded as though she was handling it all with an even temper. Trixie was the one who ultimately got her husband back, after all," said Beatrice. "Do you know much about Trixie?"

Meadow shrugged. "You know how it is here. I've definitely heard things through the years. One thing I've always noticed was that Elias and Trixie seemed to have a real love affair. I've seen them out together at the diner or at the grocery store and they're always holding hands."

Beatrice frowned. "They're newlyweds?"

"That's just it—they're not. They've been married for probably upwards of fifteen years. They just have that kind of relationship," said Meadow.

"And what do you think of Trixie personally?" asked Beatrice.

Meadow said, "She's a tough cookie. I mean, she tones it down around customers because making customers happy is her livelihood. But she definitely likes getting her own way. You probably didn't know this, but Trixie used to have a business partner who was a co-owner in the salon. That's how she'd originally been able to finance the place to begin with. Property downtown is expensive to rent, you know? And it's not cheap to get all the equipment you need for a salon."

Beatrice said, "There's no co-owner anymore, I'm guessing?"

"That's right. Because Trixie and she argued all the time over the direction of the salon. Trixie told me that they couldn't agree on *anything*—not even the types of posts they'd run on social media," said Meadow.

"Did the other woman just quit?" asked Beatrice.

"Nope. Trixie bought her out," said Meadow with a shrug. "Had to use some of Elias's money from the plumbing business to do it, but I bet he wanted to make sure to keep Trixie happy. It's sort of like the old expression . . . if Mama ain't happy, ain't nobody happy."

"You're saying that Trixie could have been a little more upset than she seemed about Elias's affair—and directed it toward Annabelle," said Beatrice.

Meadow said, "It's definitely a possibility. And, much as I like Devlin, he's a suspect, too."

"Right. Because he clearly wasn't over their relationship. He was still really choked up over Annabelle's death. If he waved to Arnold, then he must have realized he was out of the house and that Annabelle was alone. He decided it would be the perfect opportunity to plead with Annabelle to divorce her husband and start seeing him again. Maybe he lost control when she said no," said Beatrice with a shrug.

"Stabbing her with a sword?" Meadow shivered. "I don't know—it's just hard for me to picture that."

"It's hard for you to picture *anyone* in Dappled Hills doing it," said Beatrice.

"True. Which is why having Arnold Tremont responsible seems like the best option," said Meadow as she pulled into Beatrice's driveway. They smiled as Noo-noo, hearing the van, popped up in the picture window and grinned at them, cocking her head to one side fetchingly.

Beatrice said, "And the spouse is always considered the most-likely suspect."

"Right. Except that I can't really see *him* stabbing his wife, either. I know what you're going to say," said Meadow, holding up a hand. "But he's just so dignified. He also seemed kind, unlike his wife. And you could tell he really loved her. After all, the whole reason he was in town was to try to win her back."

"Arnold was always a nice guy when I saw him at events in Atlanta," said Beatrice. "I'd always prefer hanging out with him over Annabelle, if I had the option. But the facts are pretty troubling, aren't they? He decided that he wasn't ready to divorce Annabelle, despite their separate lives. You're looking at it as if he was trying to win her back, but maybe he lashed out when she didn't share his vision of a life together. They'd also apparently had that argument last night. Arnold admitted that the whole reason he took Barney for a walk was to cool off."

"Do you think that the fact that he wanted Annabelle back was also a financial decision somehow?" asked Meadow, puckering her brow. "Divorces are super-expensive."

"I think Arnold Tremont has all the money he needs. I'd be shocked if he had any sort of financial problems at all. But I do think that he's the kind of man who really hates to *lose*. And I believe he'd consider the end of his marriage to be a loss, maybe even something that looks like a personal failure," said Beatrice.

Meadow said, "So you think he came back from his long walk with his dog, tried to convince Annabelle not to divorce him, and then lost it?"

Beatrice said, "It's possible. The police certainly aren't letting him leave yet, so it's something they're considering, too."

Meadow sighed. "It feels like we haven't made much progress."

"Actually, we've made a *lot* of progress. It's just the fact that we haven't figured out which of our suspects has done it." Beatrice took off her seatbelt and saw Noo-noo jump up and put her paws on the glass window.

Meadow said, "Who do you think we should try to talk to tomorrow? You know that I want to clear Dappled Hills of any killers."

Beatrice said with a smile, "While I appreciate your concern about town safety, your husband *is* in charge of law and order and seems to do a great job of that. Here's what I'm thinking. Tomorrow is Sunday and I need to be at church with Wyatt. After that, we're supposed to head over to the retirement home to eat lunch with some of the residents there."

"And *then* we'll go out and talk to some folks?" asked Meadow eagerly.

Beatrice shook her head. "Then I think it'll be about time for me to take an afternoon nap. The food at that dining hall is super-heavy on Sundays. Besides, I still have that book of Wyatt's and I'd like to make a little more headway with it."

Meadow stared at her in horror. "That ghastly biography of John Wesley?"

"The ghastly biography of John *Calvin*," corrected Beatrice dryly. "Unfortunately, it appears to be an undocumented sleep aid, so I haven't been able to get too far with it."

"I would think not!" said Meadow. "Well, when you finally give up on it, I can recommend some stuff that actually provides a real *escape*."

Beatrice, who had already encountered a sample of what Meadow termed 'escape literature,' quickly hopped out of the car. "Maybe another time. I'm going to give this one another try."

"All right. See you at church. And don't forget the guild meeting on Monday! Remember we have a special activity," said Meadow, giving a friendly toot of the horn as she backed the car up. The friendly toot succeeded in making Noo-noo crupt in a frenzy of barking.

Chapter Eight

Sunday started out as Beatrice expected. Neither she nor Wyatt had been able to sleep very long on Saturday night and had woken up at four-thirty in the morning for good. Noo-noo gave Beatrice a bewildered look as if she'd made some sort of dreadful error in judgment getting up when it was dark outside.

But as much as Beatrice figured she'd pay for the lack of sleep later, there was something wonderful, and very unusual, in not having to rush on a Sunday morning. The newspaper was, remarkably, already in the driveway and they settled down with a pot of rather black coffee at their kitchen table. After they'd built up an appetite, Wyatt cooked a breakfast to rival even Meadow's. By the time Beatrice had eaten it all, she felt as though she could conceivably go back to bed.

"The problem now is that my tummy is so full that I'm sleepy. Why couldn't I have been sleepy at 4:30 this morning when the rest of the town was sleeping?" asked Beatrice.

Wyatt was already in his suit and carefully tying his tie in front of a mirror in the living room. "Hopefully my sermon will be riveting enough to keep you awake," he said teasingly. "If the minister's wife can't keep from nodding off, there's no hope for the rest of the congregation."

Beatrice said, "At this point, I'm worried that even if the service consists of a brass horn section blasting at full volume, it may not keep me awake."

Fortunately, she *was* able to shake it off and Wyatt's sermon, as usual, was thoughtful—and thinking helped keep her from nodding off, too.

Before they left the church, Edgenora sidled up to them at the sanctuary door. She had a concerned expression on her face.

"Everything all right?" asked Wyatt, frowning.

Edgenora said, "It's okay, but there was one thing I thought you should know. Remember how you suggested that Savannah watch the nursery for yesterday's exercise classes?"

"How did that go?" asked Beatrice. She suddenly had the sinking feeling that perhaps Savannah hadn't been the best candidate for watching small children. Savannah's brisk manner and very exacting nature may not have been a good fit for nursery duty.

Edgenora sighed. "Well, it was a success in the respect that no one was injured in the course of her shift. But that's hardly a rousing success, is it? The fact is that the children didn't seem to be having much fun."

"Why is that?" asked Wyatt.

Edgenora said, "Much as I know and love Savannah, I have to admit that she has particular traits that may not be a good match for working with small kids. For one thing, when the children were all coloring, Savannah was trying to make sure they all colored within the lines."

"How old were these kids?" asked Beatrice.

Wyatt said ruefully, "I think we put her in the toddler room."

Beatrice said, "Ah. An age group that might not just color outside the lines but possibly even tear up the coloring sheet."

Edgenora chuckled. "Right. And that was just one example. I don't believe Savannah nor the children enjoyed themselves."

Wyatt said thoughtfully, "So a change of assignment is in order. You know, Savannah would probably do a great job with our group that visits the retirement homes."

Edgenora said, "I'm sure she probably would. But unfortunately, she found a new area of interest."

"Unfortunately? Uh-oh," said Beatrice ruefully. "The only area that I can think of where that reaction may come into play is . . ."

"The choir," said Edgenora, making a face. "One of the choir members was picking up her child from the nursery and invited Savannah to join the choir."

Beatrice laughed. "Maybe just to get Savannah out of the nursery."

Wyatt said, "Are we sure that Savannah doesn't sing well? I've never heard her sing."

Edgenora said succinctly, "She croaks like a frog. The problem is that she's also tone-deaf and seems to believe that she sings well. So her *volume* is also a problem."

Wyatt said, "That's going to be for the choir director to figure out. She's been there forever and does a great job managing lots of different voices, talents, and personalities. I'm sure it will be fine."

Beatrice said, "The choir doesn't hold auditions?"

"No. Everyone is welcome to join, especially with a choir our size," said Wyatt.

Beatrice said, "Maybe I'll mention to her that the church could use a volunteer for the Tuesday evening retirement home visits."

Wyatt said, "Of course, Savannah may decide that she can do both."

Edgenora smiled. "But she wouldn't be able to. The retirement home visits conflict with choir practice."

"I'll bring it up the next time I see her," said Beatrice.

Wyatt and Beatrice left for their own retirement home visit, which simply involved visits and lunch (the Tuesday visits involved Scrabble, chess, checkers, dinner, and movie showings).

It was around two p.m. when Beatrice and Wyatt returned to the cottage to see Noo-noo's grinning face in the front window.

"Do you think she's there the whole time we're gone?" asked Wyatt. "Poor little girl."

"I think she just likes the window," said Beatrice. "She can watch the street and make sure there are no intruders. Plus, she's fond of barking at the doves and there have been quite a few at the birdfeeder lately."

Wyatt nodded and yawned. "Should I give her a quick walk before we take that nap? She might have been asleep the whole time and ready to stretch her legs."

"It wouldn't hurt," said Beatrice. "But don't worry about making it a long one. I can take her out after supper tonight for another walk."

Wyatt left with Noo-noo, whose short legs almost seemed to be skipping with delight. Beatrice picked up the biography of Calvin with a sigh. Maybe, if she sat in the most uncomfortable chair they had, she'd be able to make it through a few pages before dropping off to sleep.

She was midway through the first page when the phone rang. Beatrice answered it and heard a grumble on the other end. "Miss Sissy? Is that you?"

"Want to talk to Wyatt," said Miss Sissy, with no preamble.

"He's walking Noo-noo right now. He should be back any second. Can I get him to call you when he comes back in?"

"Just tell him to come over," snapped Miss Sissy and then Beatrice heard a *click* as she hung up.

Although Beatrice was getting used to a lot of the demands of being a minister's wife, dealing with Miss Sissy on a more-regular basis than she had as a single woman was definitely an adjustment. Wyatt was sort of a security blanket for the old woman and whenever she had any sort of problems, from a burned-out lightbulb in a ceiling fixture to just wanting to talk with someone, she gave him a call. Even though it was sometimes exasperating for Beatrice, she was glad that Miss Sissy had someone like Wyatt to turn to. Beatrice had learned since moving here that the old woman could also have a softer and warmer side.

Minutes later, Wyatt and a happy, panting Noo-noo came back into the house.

"Naptime," said Wyatt with a smile.

Beatrice winced at him. "I'm afraid not. At least, not yet. Miss Sissy called and asked for you to go over there."

Wyatt frowned. "Uh-oh. Any indication why?"

"None. She was even more abrupt than she usually is. And you know how she is normally," said Beatrice with a sigh.

"Do you think this is a pastoral visit? Or the type of visit where I need to take my toolbox?" asked Wyatt. Then he shook his head quickly, "Never mind, I'll just walk over there really quick with a toolbox and a Bible. That should cover anything." He gave her a grin.

"You're a better person than I am," said Beatrice, reaching out to give him a quick kiss. "Good luck."

Beatrice had every intention of staying awake until Wyatt came back home, but nodded off while reading the book, even while sitting in the uncomfortable wooden chair. She jumped when the front door opened again and blinked at the clock. "You've been over there for a couple of hours! What was wrong?"

Wyatt shook his head. "Honestly, I'm not certain. I could tell that *something* was on her mind, for sure. But she didn't need to have anything repaired or replaced. Something was bothering her, but she was being very careful not to tell me. At any rate, she seemed relieved when I arrived and then smiled at me during the visit, so that was a good sign. Maybe we should check on her again tomorrow."

"Good idea. Maybe she doesn't feel well and is one of those folks who doesn't like going to the doctor."

"That could be. Even more reason to check in on her." He smiled at her. "Did you get a good nap in?"

"Well, it was an accidental one," said Beatrice dryly. "I was planning on staying up until you came back. But I fell asleep in this chair and now I have a crick in my neck."

"And it's too close to bedtime for me to take a nap, myself, now," said Wyatt ruefully. "I'll just turn in early tonight."

The next morning, they arose at a more normal time. When Wyatt came home for lunch, Beatrice suddenly remembered that although she was very well aware that it was a special guild meeting, she couldn't remember *why* it was special.

As they were getting ready, Wyatt asked, "Is there a speaker at the meeting today?"

Beatrice frowned. "This isn't like me, but I can't for the life of me remember what *is* special about the meeting today except for the fact that it's at the Patchwork Cottage. It could be that we have a speaker. But it *could* be that I was supposed to do something to prepare for this meeting. And I haven't done anything."

Wyatt said, "Are you supposed to bring what you're working on now?"

"I don't think so. We frequently do that, so it wouldn't necessarily qualify as special. Oh, now it's going to bother me. I'll text someone and ask," said Beatrice, pulling out her phone.

"Meadow?" asked Wyatt as he absently looked around for his computer.

"No, Meadow will fuss too much that I didn't remember the Special Thing. And I don't want to bother Georgia since she's having such a tough time. And Posy will be busy setting up for everybody. I'll ask Savannah."

Savannah texted promptly back and Beatrice frowned. "A brown bag challenge. Not that I have any idea what that is."

Wyatt said, "It sounds like you bring your lunch in a brown paper bag."

Beatrice grinned at him. "No, I don't think that's it. Part of the fun at the guild meetings is eating, and the eating is definitely not the kind of stuff that goes into brown paper bags. Oh good, Savannah's actually offering some sort of explanation." She peered at her phone. "Apparently we put some fabric in a brown paper bag and someone else gets it."

Wyatt, who found his computer, gave Beatrice a light kiss and headed for the door. "That still sounds confusing to me. Hope you can figure it all out."

Beatrice sighed. "I guess I'll just put the fabric in and find out later. At least I wasn't supposed to prepare any more than that or else I'd really be in a jam. Oh, and I'll check in with Miss Sissy and see if she wants a ride to the Patchwork Cottage. At least I can keep her off the roads that way since she's such a holy terror in the car."

Miss Sissy looked displeased at seeing Beatrice at her door.

"Miss Sissy, I thought I'd give you a ride over to the shop," said Beatrice in as pleasant a voice as she could muster. "Besides, maybe you can tell me more about the brown paper bag project."

Miss Sissy gave a deep sigh as if her problems were legion and then she picked up her own brown paper bag and motioned for them to head to the car.

Apparently, Miss Sissy was determined to maintain a code of silence throughout the short drive. Beatrice finally decided to break the silence. She gave the old woman a smile and said, "Take a look in my bag and see what you think."

Miss Sissy gave her a scandalized look. "Not allowed," she growled.

"Oh, so the material is supposed to be a *secret*," said Beatrice. "Got it. It's taking me a while to catch on."

Miss Sissy snorted in agreement.

When Beatrice arrived at the guild meeting, she was glad that she hadn't eaten lunch before she arrived. Posy had put out mini grilled cheese sandwiches, chicken salad roll-up wraps, and devilled eggs. She also had an array of sweets, including chocolate chip cookies and sweet rolls. There was also a pound cake that was already cut up for everyone to enjoy. As Beatrice had told Wyatt, food was an integral part of the Village Quilters' meetings. Beatrice had fully expected Miss Sissy to pounce on the food and frowned when the old woman made herself a small plate and picked halfheartedly at it.

They all visited at the start of the meeting and while they ate. Posy had to jump up a few times to help customers although she had an employee there to check folks out. Sometimes, for the quilters, only Posy would do. And Posy always delivered with a smile or a tip for approaching a project. Plus, Posy knew where all the newest fabrics were and could point them out in seconds. Beatrice sidled up to Savannah.

"How is everything going?" she asked.

Savannah shifted on her feet. "It's okay. I volunteered on Saturday for the nursery. You know, the one for the yoga class and the aerobics classes."

"How did that go?" asked Beatrice, preferring for Savannah to bring it up.

Savannah sighed. "I haven't had a lot of experience with little kids. I'm not sure that it worked out so well. Maybe it's not the best place for me to volunteer."

Beatrice said, "Wyatt had another idea and another group that needs a helping hand. There's a Tuesday evening group that goes from the church to different retirement homes each week."

Savannah said, "Really? What do they do there? Just talk?"

Conversation was not necessarily Savannah's forte, either. "They do talk, but they also have activities. They play Scrabble, chess, and checkers. Sometimes they'll watch movies," said Beatrice.

Savannah nodded in a considering manner. "The thing is, I was looking at joining the church choir. Tuesday is when the choir practices."

Beatrice said, "But the group sings sometimes, too, if you're interested in singing. They do Christmas carols and sing for Easter, too. It's just that they're not *always* singing."

Savannah said, "I'll give it a try tomorrow, then."

"Perfect! I'll let Wyatt know. And here's the contact information for the lady who's in charge of the group," said Beatrice, jotting down an email address and name and handing it over to Savannah.

Savannah smiled in a pleased way and stored the piece of paper carefully in her purse. She looked up as the shop bell rang. It was her sister Georgia, looking a bit frazzled. Savannah clicked her tongue and said to Beatrice, "She's trying to do too much."

Beatrice said, "At least she made it. She'd told Meadow and me that she didn't think she could come. And she probably had to wrap up things at the school after the students were dismissed and before she came here."

Savannah sighed. "I wish that I could help her out. She always has so much work to do. She's let me do a little grading from time to time, but there's only so much of that I can do. She'll only have me work on the kind of grading that has an answer key. If there's anything subjective, she feels like she needs to do it herself."

Edgenora came up to ask Savannah something and Beatrice made her way over to Georgia. Meadow, who had also noticed Georgia's arrival, did the same.

Georgia flushed. "Sorry I'm running behind. I know I told you that I wasn't going to be able to make it, but I wanted to come enough to squeeze it in. I wanted to take care of some grading at school before I left. But I especially wanted to make the meeting since I'm not sure if I'll be able to come to one for a while . . . if I end up getting a second job."

Meadow said to Beatrice, "Are you thinking what I'm thinking?"

Beatrice, never one to try to guess what might be on Meadow's mind, shook her head.

Meadow held up her hands, showing off her nail color. "Clearly, this isn't going to be a solution to the problems you're facing right now. But the fact is that you need a break. I know you don't have a lot of time, but Beatrice and I were saying how relaxed and rejuvenated we felt after we got our nails done at Trixie's shop."

Georgia looked at Beatrice with interest. "You went too?"

Beatrice nodded. "As unlikely as that sounds, I did. I have to admit that Trixie did a great job."

Meadow said, "And the other girl who works there is good, too. Anyway, I've been trying to think of ways to help you out and I would like to gift you the manicure."

Beatrice said, scrabbling in her purse, "Put me down for half."

Georgia's eyes teared up, alarming Beatrice, as she took their cash. But she just said, "Thank you. That sounds amazing."

Meadow gave her a hug. "Sometimes we just have to take the time to do something just for ourselves."

Beatrice nodded. "I always forced myself to take some kind of break even when things were crazy in Atlanta. If you don't, it's going to catch up with you."

Georgia gave them a grateful look. "I'm going to look forward to a break."

Their conversation was interrupted by Posy, gently trying to herd her quilters into the back room where their program was to be conducted. Everyone sat down, still holding their brown paper bags. Beatrice looked curiously at Miss Sissy, who usually would continue to eat throughout the meeting. Miss Sissy glared back at her.

After some guild business was discussed and future events mentioned, Posy said with her eyes sparkling, "Now it's time for the brown bags! If you take a bag, please make sure you have the time to complete the project by Christmas. But don't feel as though you need to take one if you're not sure you have time." This with a concerned look at Georgia.

Beatrice raised her hand and said wryly, "At the risk of sounding like I haven't been paying attention, could you explain more what the brown bag challenge actually *is*?"

Miss Sissy, who had finally left the refreshment table, glared at her and muttered under her breath. Whatever it was, Beatrice was sure it wasn't complimentary.

Posy covered her mouth with one hand. "Oops! Sorry, I should have explained that."

Miss Sissy growled, "Everybody else knows it."

Posy continued, "Whoever wants to participate will draw a bag. Each bag has a number on it and every number corresponds to the quilter who filled the bag. I keep note of who has whose bag. Whoever participates *must* make something with the fabric inside before our Christmas party deadline. Then the project goes back to the original quilter who put the fabric in the bag."

Meadow said, "It's like a gift for the quilter who filled the bag."

Savannah made a face. "And there really aren't any other rules."

"Which is tough for someone like Savannah who likes more structure," said her sister, grinning.

Posy said, "You could use the fabric for any number of things. It could be a lap blanket, or a pillow, or a Christmas stocking, or whatever you like."

Beatrice said, "What if there isn't enough fabric to make what we want to make?"

"That sounds ambitious," said Meadow with a grin.

Posy said, "You can add fabric to it, but you have to use at least some of the fabric in the project."

Beatrice said, "Sounds like a real creative challenge."

Meadow said, "And it's *fun*. So let's all draw."

Everyone ended up exchanging bags, even Georgia. But Beatrice knew that Georgia worked so quickly that she could come up with something great even if she *didn't* have enough time.

Meadow was eating a few more snacks when her phone rang. She frowned and stepped to the far end of the shop so that she could hear the conversation. A few minutes later she came back and pulled Beatrice away.

"What's wrong?" asked Beatrice in a low voice.

"It's Devlin Wilson," said Meadow, an angry flush starting up from her neck. "He's dead!"

Chapter Nine

Moments later Meadow and Beatrice were heading to their respective cars in the Patchwork Cottage parking lot. Beatrice had quietly asked Posy if she could take Miss Sissy back home for her. They didn't say a word to anyone else on the way out and no one noticed that they were slipping out since the meeting was in the process of ending, anyway.

Beatrice said, "Ramsay may not want us to be anywhere around his crime scene, you know."

Meadow sniffed. "If he knows what's good for him, he'll let us be in the area. I want you to find out exactly what's going on here before things get even worse! Besides, he *did* call me."

"To let you know that he wouldn't be home for dinner," said Beatrice in a dry voice. "That's hardly the same thing as inviting you to come out to interfere with a murder investigation."

"Regardless, we're going," said Meadow, slamming her car door with determination.

Soon they were pulling in at the curb on the street that Devlin Wilson had lived on. A street that was now full of emergency vehicles.

Beatrice and Meadow got out of their cars and watched silently as the police, in their forensic gear, appeared to be hovering around one particular area of Devlin's yard.

Meadow said, "Look, there's Goldie."

Goldie Parson had already spotted them and was heading over. When she reached them, Beatrice could see that her eyes were red from crying and her blonde ponytail was mussed. She wordlessly gave them hugs and held back her sobs.

Beatrice asked softly, "What on earth happened, Goldie?"

She blinked hard, swallowed, and then said, "I was on my way to visit with him. Devlin. You know, about the downtown initiative, since his office is down there. He hadn't been in the office this afternoon, and I was passing by here anyway, so I thought I'd drop by his house. I was ringing his doorbell, and he wasn't coming, even though his car was in the driveway. I thought that was sort of odd. I knocked at the door and he didn't come. Then I happened to glance over in the side yard." She bobbed her head to indicate the spot where the police were gathered.

Meadow's eyes were huge. "And you saw him?"

Goldie nodded. "I guess I had been so focused on what I was going to tell him that I didn't even notice." She shivered.

Beatrice asked, "What had happened to him?"

Goldie said, "Well, you know he's been working on that massive yard project of his for weeks now."

Beatrice nodded. "Yes, he'd told me about it. Said it was sort of like therapy for him—to go outside and do yardwork."

Goldie said, "He has all of these big stones in his yard that he's using for garden pavers. At first when I saw him, it almost looked like he was taking a nap in his yard. He was crumpled, but I thought he looked kind of curled up like you do when you nap. It looked like he was wearing earbuds to listen to music, even. I went over there and I was going to tease him about taking an afternoon siesta in his yard."

Meadow said breathlessly, "But when you got closer, you could tell he was dead."

Goldie nodded wordlessly.

Beatrice said, "It sounds as if you've been out all morning. Was there anything that you noticed, anything that didn't seem right? Perhaps someone leaving this street?"

Goldie sighed. "I'm just super-frustrated with myself right now. After all, I'm the person who was so unobservant that I didn't even see a body in the yard when I walked up the walkway!"

Beatrice noticed that she didn't look at her though. Beatrice said slowly, "Are you sure? Even if you saw something that seems to be totally unimportant, maybe it plays a part in what happened here today."

Goldie took a deep breath and looked back up at Beatrice. "I did see someone leaving Devlin's property. But I'm sure it had nothing to do with this. He was probably here the same as I was—with some sort of business."

"He?" asked Meadow.

"Arnold," said Goldie in a reluctant tone. "I saw Arnold Tremont leaving as I was coming in."

"Leaving the street or leaving the property?" asked Beatrice.

"The property," said Goldie. "But, like I said, he might have had good reason to have been here, like I did."

"Maybe he wanted to get in touch with Devlin to sell the house," said Meadow. "After all, he was packing when we were there. He sure isn't planning on sticking around. And Devlin is the best agent in town. Or, well, he *was*."

Beatrice said, "But why wouldn't he have just picked up the phone and called him?"

Goldie shrugged. "Maybe he was restless or was tired of packing. Maybe he needed to walk and stretch his legs and clear his head."

It sounded as if those things were on Goldie's list, as well.

Beatrice said, "Maybe so. Did you see anyone else besides Arnold?"

Goldie quickly shook her head, avoiding Beatrice's eyes.

Beatrice said, "I hate to bring this up, Goldie, but someone mentioned that you might have been more upset with Annabelle than you let on."

Goldie blinked at Beatrice for a few moments and then sighed. "I truly do love Dappled Hills. I only wish that residents were able to keep from gossiping over every little thing. As I told Ramsay, it *stung* when Annabelle sneered at my efforts in a public forum. But it didn't set me on some sort of murderous path. I wasn't *homicidal*. Besides, as I mentioned, I really did want to pick her brain for ideas for making Dappled Hills a better place."

She turned as her name was called by one of the police officers. "Looks like they want to talk to me again. Excuse me."

Goldie walked away towards the police officer and Meadow said with her hands on her hips, "Well, this has turned into quite the mess."

Beatrice said, "Shouldn't we leave now? Besides, it's getting close to dinner. Wyatt will start wondering what type of marathon guild meeting we're having at the Patchwork Cottage."

Meadow said, "Send him a text. I want to wait until Ramsay comes over and gives us a little more information about all this. Besides, he'll want to know what you think, Beatrice."

Beatrice said wryly, "I'm not sure that he will. He does have a forensics team and a lot more incoming information than we do, Meadow."

"Then how is it that you're always the one who figures out the murderer?" asked Meadow. She peered at the group of police. "Look, he's heading over here now!"

Ramsay was starting to look tired. He said, "I thought y'all were at a guild meeting with Posy. Although I have to ask myself why I'm not really surprised that you two are over here?"

Meadow said tartly, "You should have known when you phoned me that I'd be over here in a jiffy with Beatrice."

"What happened here?" asked Beatrice to Ramsay.

He rubbed his face and sighed. "Well, it sure looks like somebody got rid of poor Devlin Wilson because he knew something. I can't think of any other reason why someone would take him down. Although what he knew, I have no idea. He sure didn't share it with me. Somebody must have been feeling pretty desperate to come up, hit Devlin on the head with a paver in bright daylight, and then get on their way."

Beatrice frowned. "He didn't seem like the kind of guy who would blackmail someone."

Ramsay shrugged. "He wouldn't have to. What if he'd simply *seen* something? After all, he was over there in the neighborhood at the time of Annabelle's murder. He might have seen something and just not been real sure about what he saw. Then the murderer decides not to take a chance that he might say something and just takes him out, too."

Meadow said, "It did sound like he was paying a lot of attention to Annabelle's house instead of the showing he was supposed to be giving. But then, I guess he was still in love with her."

"The funny thing was that he already *said* that he'd seen someone there. Arnold Tremont," said Beatrice.

"We're working under the assumption that Arnold isn't the one who killed Devlin," said Ramsay. "But who knows? Maybe Devlin saw more than he let on about Arnold, and Arnold wanted to ensure his silence," said Ramsay.

Beatrice said, "Goldie did mention to us that she saw Arnold leaving the property."

Ramsay nodded. "She told us the same thing. Sure is looking like the husband did it after all."

Beatrice glanced over at the forensics team in Devlin's yard. "And no one saw anything? In the front yard?"

Ramsay shook his head. "We've already gone around knocking on doors and no one saw a thing. For a town that knows everyone's business, that's pretty amazing. Although I will say that even Goldie didn't notice anything, and she walked right up to Devlin's front door."

Beatrice said, "It *is* a very shady spot, and he was obviously lying very still. I'm not sure anyone would really notice unless they were specifically looking for something in his front yard."

Her phone buzzed at her in the pocket of her khaki slacks. She made a face. "I have the feeling that's Wyatt. I should have let him know where I am."

Ramsay said dryly, "Tell him you're perfectly safe at a crime scene." He headed back toward the group of policemen. "Meadow, I'll see you sometime tonight. Hopefully."

It was Wyatt on the phone. "Everything okay?" he asked with concern.

"I'm fine, but Devlin Wilson is dead," said Beatrice. "Meadow is here with me and we've been talking with Ramsay. I'll fill you in when I come home."

After she'd ended the call, Beatrice said, "I should probably let Piper know, too." She called Piper and broke the news as gently as she could, but Piper still sounded shocked. Even though Devlin hadn't been a friend, she and Ash had still been seeing a lot of him in the last few weeks.

When she hung up, Meadow said, "What a mess. I know Piper was sorry to hear about Devlin. Should we get an early start tomorrow? I'm not even sure I'll be able to sleep tonight, especially since Ramsay probably won't be there most of the time. I have a tough time sleeping when he's not there."

"I could lend you my Calvin biography," said Beatrice with a smile.

"No thank you! I'd rather just skip a little sleep. So back to tomorrow. Who do you want to start out speaking with?"

Beatrice said, "Ordinarily, I'd say Arnold. But if we have an early start, it wouldn't be right to go over to his house and wake him up. I have a feeling that he's staying up late with the packing. Maybe we should see Trixie."

Meadow peered at Beatrice's hands. "I think that's a good idea anyway, considering that you've chipped your nails in several places. What have you been doing? Yardwork?"

Beatrice grimaced as she looked at her fingers. "I'm just not used to having them painted. You're right; they look like a disaster."

Meadow said, "And Trixie's nail salon doesn't open *that* early. I think it opens at ten. But still, I don't want to be at the house by myself. How about if we go to breakfast before we head over to Trixie's? And have Wyatt come with us before he heads to work? I don't want to steal you all for myself."

Beatrice nodded. "That sounds perfect. See you at nine?"

When Beatrice got home, she found that Noo-noo had been fed, the house had been tidied up, and Wyatt had made spaghetti and meatballs with garlic bread. Not only that, but he had a glass of wine ready for her.

"You're too good to be true," said Beatrice, taking a sip of her wine and reaching down to pet Noo-noo, who instantly rolled on her back for a tummy rub, tilting her head to one side and grinning up at Beatrice.

Wyatt smiled at her. "It sounded like you had a rough day." He frowned. "You weren't the one who found poor Devlin, were you?"

"No, fortunately. Goldie did. It was a weird day," said Beatrice, cutting up a meatball. "Everything seemed completely normal at first. We had a good guild meeting and I actually finally learned what a brown bag exchange was. But then Meadow got a phone call at the end of the meeting from Ramsay about Devlin."

Wyatt chuckled. "Then he must not have been worried about keeping the information quiet."

"You know how it is in Dappled Hills—the news was probably on its way out, anyway," said Beatrice with a shrug. "But no, I think his intent was to let Meadow know that he wasn't going to be home for supper."

Wyatt scooped some spaghetti on Beatrice's plate and sprinkled it with Parmesan cheese. "At least you weren't the one to find Devlin."

Beatrice shook her head. "No. Goldie was looking for Devlin to loop him in on the downtown initiative." She sighed. "I feel so sorry for him. He was in bad shape when Meadow and I saw him at Cork's wine shop. Cork said he'd become a very regular customer. He seemed to be distraught over Annabelle's death and it also looked like he hadn't gotten over their breakup. He'd mentioned that he was doing a lot of yardwork to keep himself distracted. Then this happens." Beatrice shrugged.

"Did Ramsay give any info that could help explain why Devlin was murdered?" asked Wyatt, taking a bite of his spaghetti. Noo-noo sat on the floor next to him, watching intently and clearly hoping that Wyatt would be clumsy enough to drop something and truly make the evening memorable for her.

"Not really. He seemed to think that it was possible that Devlin knew something that the killer wanted to keep quiet," said Beatrice. "And Devlin admitted to being across from the house when Annabelle was murdered, so maybe he did. But Ramsay said that he didn't tell him anything."

Wyatt said, "What's your plan for tomorrow?"

Beatrice said, "We'll start talking to folks again. We might see Trixie first since Meadow wanted to get an early start and get out of the house. Oh, and Meadow invited us to have breakfast tomorrow morning before we head to the nail salon."

Wyatt said regretfully, "I'd usually love to go, but I have the men's prayer breakfast tomorrow morning."

Beatrice said, "Ugh, I'd totally forgotten that. This is what happens—I get so involved in trying to figure this stuff out that I lose track of everything else."

"At least you made the guild meeting and figured out the paper bag project," said Wyatt teasingly.

"Got to keep track of the big stuff," said Beatrice with a grin.

The next morning, Beatrice set off after Wyatt left for the prayer breakfast. The restaurant was in an old building in downtown Dappled Hills. The original brick walls and tin ceiling gave it atmosphere and the smell of pancakes and sausage made Beatrice's mouth water. It was a good combination.

Meadow raised her eyebrows when Beatrice came into the restaurant alone. "Where's Wyatt?"

"Prayer breakfast," said Beatrice succinctly as she slid her chair out.

Meadow said, "Wow, I'd totally forgotten what day of the week it is."

"Apparently, that's contagious," said Beatrice. "I'd lost track of time, myself."

They ordered their plates, which came rapidly. Meadow went with the pancake breakfast with blackberries on top and Beatrice had the three-egg breakfast with sides of grits, turkey sausage, and toast and jam.

As soon as they were done, Meadow said, "Want to walk over to Trixie's? We may as well leave our cars when we can and it's not a bad day out there today."

"Sounds good."

A few minutes later, they were over at Trixie's salon. Fortunately, it wasn't busy in there and Trixie looked up and greeted them as soon as they came in. She didn't seem quite as pleased to see them as she had when they'd come in earlier.

"Was there a problem with the manicures, ladies?" she asked, looking very much as if she hoped that wasn't the case.

Beatrice said, "No problem except with me. I'm not used to having my nails painted and I've chipped them pretty badly. If you can fill them in, I'll try to be more careful."

Meadow laughed. "Or maybe wear gloves."

Trixie relaxed a little. "I can fix that for you." She gave Beatrice a sideways glance. "I'm surprised that you weren't used to manicures. Weren't you in some kind of fancy business in Atlanta?"

Beatrice gave a short laugh. "I don't know about *fancy*. I was an art museum curator. Everyone was paying more attention to the art than they were to my nails. I just always kept them short and neat."

Trixie studied her nails and then walked to the wall where the polishes were displayed. "I think this is the right color," she said, shaking the bottle and then holding it out for Beatrice to see.

Beatrice said, "It looks like it. Thanks."

They sat down at a table and Trixie said in a casual voice, "So I guess y'all heard about Devlin Wilson's death."

Meadow said, "We sure have. Poor guy."

Trixie gave a laconic shrug. "Somebody did him in for a reason. Maybe he wasn't such a poor guy after all. Who knows what was going on?"

Beatrice said, "Then you don't think the two recent deaths are connected?"

Trixie said, "Again, who knows? Maybe they are, maybe they aren't. It makes you think, though, doesn't it? Maybe they were both done by her husband." Her mouth twisted into a smile as though this thought was pleasing to her.

"What do you mean?" asked Beatrice.

"Well, he was probably upset that his wife was seeing other men, right? I mean, what husband wouldn't be?" asked Trixie.

Meadow said, "But they were separated. They were barely even seeing each other. And Beatrice says that they were even living that way when she knew them in Atlanta."

Trixie shrugged again. "Yeah, but maybe he wasn't planning on giving his wife up altogether. That happens, you know? Anyway, so maybe the husband finds out his wife is messing around on him and kills her. Then he goes after the guy that she was messing around *with*."

Beatrice said delicately, "But, if that were the case, wouldn't he also be going after your husband?"

"Elias?" Trixie snorted. "Why on earth would he do that? That relationship is over, believe me. I think Devlin wasn't so convinced that his relationship with Annabelle was finished though. I bet he tried to convince her to come back to him and Annabelle's husband went berserk. Maybe Devlin called

Annabelle while her husband was in the house. Or maybe he even dropped by."

Meadow said in as careless a voice as she could muster, "Has Ramsay been by the shop to speak to you, Trixie?"

Trixie didn't look up from her careful focus on her handiwork. "He's been by a couple of times and the state police, too. I reckon they're just trying to cover their bases, what with Elias and all. But I told them the truth. I was at the shop working late yesterday evening and Elias was at the construction site fitting pipes until the sun went down." She stopped and looked at Beatrice's nails with a critical eye. "I think that's better, right?"

Beatrice couldn't even tell that the nails had ever been chipped. "Much better. What do I owe you?" she asked as she reached for her purse.

Both Trixie and Meadow shrieked, "Stop!" at Beatrice, making her catch her breath in her throat.

"For heaven's sake, Beatrice! You'll ruin your nails again," said Meadow, rolling her eyes. "Just sit still and I'll pull out your debit card."

So Beatrice did, watching while Meadow paid and tipped Trixie. By this time, another customer, who appeared to be a regular, had entered the salon and was chatting with Trixie. When Beatrice's nails had finally dried, they headed out the door.

Chapter Ten

Beatrice said, "That took forever."

"Yes, but we got information at the same time," said Meadow. "We killed two birds with one stone."

"What information do *you* think we heard?" asked Beatrice as they headed toward their cars.

"Well, that Trixie said she couldn't have done it because she was at the shop," said Meadow with a shrug. "Whether that's the truth or not. And that she thinks that there's some sort of soap opera type reason that Devlin was murdered. That it all has to do with a love triangle and jealousies and anger."

Beatrice said, "I guess we'll try to follow up with Arnold next."

Meadow said, "Should we bring him more food? Maybe we could say that we felt badly because he doesn't really know anyone in town and we wanted to make sure he had plenty of food."

Beatrice grinned at her. "That makes it sound as though we think Arnold is completely incapable of heating up a microwave meal or something. He's a pretty sophisticated man with a good deal of means. And he wasn't with Annabelle most of the time, so he's used to being independent. I'm sure he knows how to rustle up some food in town."

"Was he independent? It sounded to me like he really wanted to fix his marriage and not be independent at all," said Meadow. She paused. "Well, speak of the devil," she said in her stage whisper that likely carried all the *way* down the street. "It's Arnold. I guess you're right—he's in the process of getting himself brunch, it looks like. And I do believe that I'm suddenly hungry again."

Beatrice groaned. "I'm pretty sure I couldn't force anything else in my stomach after my eggs and sausage, but I suppose I could be up for a coffee."

They walked in and saw Arnold, sitting alone with a Dappled Hills newspaper at his table. He looked up when he saw them and pointed to the empty chairs near him. "Come sit with me," he said. "Every time I go into town I feel like I look like a hermit or something. No one wants to come over and talk."

They sat down and the waitress took their order for coffees. Beatrice said, "They're probably just not sure what to say. They'd need to introduce themselves and then extend sympathy. That's probably pretty tough to do during an introduction."

Arnold said, "I'm sure you're right. I'm being a little uncharitable. It's just that I'm not accustomed to being alone. Oh, and Beatrice, thanks for giving me Wyatt's information. I spoke to him yesterday about a service for Annabelle."

"That's good. Thanks for letting me know—I came home late yesterday and Wyatt didn't remember to tell me about it."

Arnold nodded, looking serious again at the reminder of Annabelle's death. He sighed. "Everything's just such a mess right now. Literally and figuratively. The house is completely trashed with my packing. And I'm still not allowed to leave town."

Beatrice asked, "Did the police extend the time they've asked you to stay here?"

Arnold nodded. "That's right. The Devlin Wilson murder."

The waitress brought the coffee over. When she'd left again, Beatrice said, "What do you make of that?"

Meadow was still agitated by the thought of Devlin's death. "What *can* you think of it? Total evil!"

Beatrice thought that Meadow was actually starting to sound like Miss Sissy.

Arnold smiled faintly and said, "I agree. Not too much to be said about it. Somebody appears to be on a rampage in this little town. I can't figure out why. Dappled Hills seems like such an innocuous place on the outside that it's hard to believe these kinds of crimes are happening here." He put some cream in his coffee. "And I think it's a shame. I *liked* Devlin."

Meadow said loyally, "He was such a great guy."

Arnold added some sweetener to the coffee and stirred it. "I'm not going to say that I wasn't upset with him about telling the cops that I'd returned to the house. But that was just some momentary frustration because I was ready to leave town. I did like the guy. He seemed very genuine and was very eager to help."

"Had you seen him at all after Annabelle's death?" asked Beatrice.

Arnold shook his head. "It wasn't for want of trying, though. I did go to Devlin's house yesterday. In fact, I saw a young woman arriving as I left, so I'm pretty sure that's been mentioned to the police."

Meadow stared at him as if she was hearing his confession. "You *went* there?"

"I sure did. I wanted to use Devlin to sell my house," said Arnold. His food was brought to the table, and he took his fork and knife out of his rolled napkin.

Meadow said in her stage whisper again, "But he had an affair with your wife!"

Arnold smiled at her. "The reminder is unnecessary. Believe me, I remember. But there were extenuating circumstances, remember? We were separated and Annabelle was pursuing a divorce. Besides, I felt sorry for the guy."

Beatrice asked, "Sorry because of how devastated he was by Annabelle's death?"

"Exactly. I felt as if he and I had something in common with that. Her death clearly affected him as strongly as it had me. I'd seen him around town and thought he looked like death warmed over." Arnold cut up a piece of sausage. "I think he was taking out his feelings on his yard. I could totally understand him wanting to throw his extra energy at a project. That's sort of what I've been doing with all the packing."

"So you decided to head over to his house," said Beatrice.

"That's right. I was out anyway, and I was worried that Devlin wouldn't pick up the phone if I called him. Understandably, he seemed to be trying to avoid me. I think he was worried that I was upset over his relationship with Annabelle. Instead, I genuinely wanted to give him the job of selling the house." He paused. "Who knows what I'm going to do about finding a real estate agent now?"

Meadow said, "And you didn't see him? When he was out in the yard?"

Arnold shook his head and finished chewing a bite of food. "I didn't. I was pretty single-mindedly focused on ringing the doorbell. He didn't answer, of course. I thought, again, that he was trying to avoid me. After all, his car was in the driveway. He was clearly at home. I just can't believe this happened to him. The guy couldn't catch a break."

Beatrice asked, "Can you think of anything you might have seen or heard to give us a clue as to who might have killed either your wife or Devlin Wilson?"

Arnold thoughtfully took a bite of eggs. After a few moments he said, "I still wonder about that Gene guy across the street."

Beatrice asked wryly, "The one who reported that you'd come back to the house on Friday night?"

Arnold made a face. "The very one. But it's not just me being vengeful. As odd as it might sound, Annabelle and I still spent a good deal of time talking on the phone and catching each other up on our days. Maybe it was habit, maybe it was something else. On my end, our conversations were something that made me think our marriage still had a chance."

Beatrice asked, "And she mentioned Gene?"

"Sure. I mean, we didn't talk about *everything*. She didn't specifically mention the different men she was seeing, just that she was seeing people. But this Gene she did mention a lot. Not romantically, but because she was really irritated with him. Beatrice, you know what Annabelle was like when she was irritated," said Arnold with a sad smile.

Beatrice nodded. She did indeed.

"So anyway, Annabelle had something of a bee in her bonnet over Gene. She felt as if he was out to get her. First, he'd tried to throw as many roadblocks up as he could when the house was being constructed. He even commissioned some kind of environmental study to see if the construction work would harm any type of endangered wildlife," said Arnold, shaking his head.

Meadow said, "Obviously nothing was found, since the house was built."

"Right. But he didn't get over it. He'd be in Annabelle's yard sometimes, she said, determined to take in the view that he used to have. She'd look out the window, and he'd be there in the back yard, sitting near the edge and looking at the view of the valley," said Arnold. "I thought it was a little crazy and told her to give the local police a call."

"Ramsay would have been happy to go over there. That's trespassing, after all," said Meadow, sounding indignant at the thought of Gene hanging out in Annabelle's yard.

"I'm sure he would have, but for some reason, Annabelle didn't want to make the phone call. She didn't see Gene as a threat, just something of a nuisance. Then, when she was having trouble getting a cell phone connection, she started petitioning for a new tower to improve the signal. But Gene was ready to shut that down too, of course. This time, though, he had some agreement from folks in the town. It didn't look like the tower was going to come to fruition and that made Annabelle annoyed, too." A smile played around Arnold's lips at the memory.

"Do you think he would have killed again, though?" asked Beatrice. "When it wasn't something he felt passionate about?"

Arnold lifted his eyebrows. "Oh, I think so. I actually saw him there at Devlin's house. Well, not *quite* at Devlin's house, but just a few houses down. He'd pulled over to the side of the street when I was leaving. He was glancing around, shifty-eyed. I thought he looked rather suspicious. Besides, I have the feeling anyone could be passionate about self-preservation."

Once Beatrice and Meadow had finished their coffees, they left Arnold with the rest of his breakfast and his newspaper.

Meadow said, "The more I see him, the more I like him. He seems so reasonable!"

"And not like someone who would kill his wife with an ancient sword?" asked Beatrice in a hushed voice. "Just remember that he may be putting on an act to protect himself, too. He was the one who brought up the self-preservation instinct."

Meadow shrugged. "Maybe. But I really can't see it."

They were walking past the Patchwork Cottage when Posy popped outside to greet them. "I was just about to call one or both of you! I'm glad I spotted you walking past the shop. Are you doing anything important?" she asked, her brows furrowed anxiously.

"Nothing that can't be put off," said Beatrice. "Is something wrong?"

Posy glanced through the shop window at the sofa in her sitting area. Beatrice and Meadow followed her gaze and saw Miss Sissy, glowering back at them through hooded eyes.

"I'd noticed that Miss Sissy has been in a really awful mood lately. I'd tried to ask her about it, but she just growled at me."

"Sounds likely. And I know just what you mean—I'd tried to find out what was bugging her, too," said Beatrice.

"Well, it turns out that Miss Sissy has a terrible toothache," said Posy. "And she's really been impossible."

"Impossible for a normal person? Or impossible for Miss Sissy?" asked Meadow, with some trepidation. Clearly, she had not planned on dealing with an obstreperous Miss Sissy today.

Posy considered this. "Impossible for Miss Sissy. But it's not really her fault when she feels so miserable. No wonder she'd been so grouchy. I finally spotted her cradling her jaw in her hand and put two and two together. I pleaded with her to go see a dentist, but she kept shaking her head. Then, when Maisie was cozying up with her on the sofa, I saw a big tear trickle down Miss Sissy's cheek. She really needs to go. She finally agreed to let me call her dentist, but they were completely booked up. I called mine and they have an available appointment in about an hour. I'd take her myself but I don't have anyone available to relieve me at the shop. I don't trust her to drive herself over there. Besides, she'd terrorize the whole town in the process."

Beatrice said, "We'll be happy to take her for you. No problem at all."

Posy beamed at them. "Thanks so much! I felt so sorry for her, but it was frustrating when she didn't want to go. I really appreciate it."

Beatrice said, "Do you want us to take her now? We're talking with a couple of people here in downtown, but she can either come with us or we can run by later and pick her up."

Meadow said, "Oh, let's take her now if she's so upset. It'll be a nice distraction for her."

Posy went in to tell Miss Sissy and Meadow groaned. "Why do I have the feeling that this is going to be our very own personal challenge today? Not that I don't feel sorry for her. When you don't have anything to do but think about how much your teeth hurt, then your teeth hurt even worse. Will we be able to talk with anybody with her around?"

Beatrice said, "I don't see why not. It's not like everyone in town isn't used to her little eccentricities. Except for Arnold, maybe, but we've already spoken with him today."

Meadow asked, "So, where are we off to now? Gene? Arnold seemed to be pretty down on him."

"Sure. Where would he most likely be now?"

"I don't know *everyone's* schedule in town, you know," said Meadow, eyes twinkling.

"But you do know Gene's?"

"I've noticed that Gene seems to be spending a good deal of time at Goldie's office," said Meadow. "Now, I'm not saying that he's definitely there now, but we could check and see."

"Are they an item?" asked Beatrice, frowning.

"You don't think they could be? The rumor around town is that they might be," said Meadow.

"I don't know. They just seem really different from each other. Gene is this sort of nerdy guy who likes stargazing and crosswords and Goldie is this sweet Girl Scout. Gene is prickly and Goldie tries to smooth things over," said Beatrice. "Goldie is warm and Gene is cold."

Meadow shrugged. "They say that opposites attract. Maybe that's the case for Gene and Goldie. I hope Goldie is happy, no matter what. She's too sweet not to be."

Posy came back out again with a sullen Miss Sissy.

"Here you are, Miss Sissy! You'll be better before you know it," said Posy kindly.

Miss Sissy growled under her breath and Posy gave her a quick hug and hurried back to her customer waiting at the cash register.

Meadow said cheerfully, "Miss Sissy, yay! We get to hang out today."

Miss Sissy glowered at her and gave a snort.

Beatrice said, "Before we take you to the dentist, we do have someone to speak with. From what Posy told us, you should have plenty of time before your appointment."

Miss Sissy's curiosity was piqued. "Who?" she asked gruffly.

"Gene Fitzsimmons," said Meadow brightly. "He's probably over in the town hall with Goldie."

Miss Sissy's eyes lit up. "Sweethearts," she said.

Meadow laughed as they headed slowly in the direction of the town hall. "Exactly. See, Beatrice? Everyone *has* heard about it."

"I still just can't see those two together," said Beatrice.

Meadow waved her hands. "It's either opposites attracting, like I was saying before, or maybe Gene is surprisingly creative and full of ideas for Dappled Hills downtown development." Her voice was doubtful on the viability of this prospect.

"Won't it look very obvious if we just walk into Goldie's office and start questioning Gene about Annabelle and Devlin? Maybe we should have an excuse to go in there," said Beatrice, always leery about looking nosy. Besides, they looked even odder than usual with the inclusion of Miss Sissy in their group.

"As it happens, I have a wonderful excuse. I've seen these cute, cartoony Town of Dappled Hills maps of downtown and I wanted to pick one up for the police station," said Meadow breezily.

Miss Sissy muttered under her breath at the thought of the cute, cartoony map. Or, possibly at the idea of making the police station a more cheerful place.

Beatrice laughed. "The police station? So the troublemakers can see where to go downtown?"

Meadow said, "Well, it would sure make the station look better. It's pretty cold and sterile right now. One of those maps would make it cheerier."

"I guess it's as good an excuse as we're likely to have," said Beatrice.

Meadow peered through the door of the Town Hall and hissed, "What did I tell you? He's in there with a bag of fried chicken and he and Goldie are *sharing* it!"

Miss Sissy perked up at the words *fried chicken*. Then her hand stole up and gently cradled her jaw and she glowered again.

Beatrice said, "I don't think Ramsay would find that to be good enough evidence to determine they're having a relationship. But let's go in instead of just standing here at the door looking suspicious."

Chapter Eleven

They walked in and Goldie blushed, jumping to her feet as if having been discovered acting unprofessionally at work. "How are you ladies doing?" she asked, a bit loudly. "Want to join us for lunch? Gene was kind enough to pick some up."

The look on Gene's face was hardly a welcoming one. Beatrice hid a smile. Clearly, he was not looking forward to sharing lunch with Goldie in any way.

Meadow said, "We're fine, but thanks!"

Miss Sissy looked longingly at the chicken and Goldie quickly asked, "Chicken for you, Miss Sissy? I have a paper plate I can pull out for you."

Miss Sissy gave the chicken a wistful look and then shook her head.

Goldie looked confused by this, as well she might, considering the fact that, in anyone's memory, Miss Sissy never turned down an opportunity to eat.

"Toothache," said Beatrice succinctly and Goldie nodded in sympathy.

"Was there anything that I could do for you ladies?" asked Goldie.

"I thought I'd pick up one of those nice Dappled Hills maps to take to the police station," said Meadow with a big smile. "The one where all the businesses are illustrated."

Gene, who had been sitting uncomfortably, now grinned. "You're wanting to beautify the police station?"

Miss Sissy rolled her eyes.

Meadow said, "Don't you think it could use it? It's not much to look at, is it?"

"It most definitely could use it, but I'm not sure Ramsay would agree," said Gene.

Meadow said, "If Ramsay had his way, the police station would resemble a library with book-lined walls and notebooks ready for poetry-writing. He just hasn't gotten around to it yet. I'm sure he'd love a Dappled Hills map in there."

Goldie opened one of the cabinets behind her and rummaged for a few seconds before pulling out a map. "Here you are. Hope it brightens up the station. I think the artist did a great job."

"Too bad the station isn't on the map," said Gene with a chuckle.

Goldie smiled at him, "I guess it didn't really fit in with the vision of what we were trying to accomplish." Her phone rang, and she glanced at it. "Sorry, but I've got to take this." She disappeared into a back room.

Gene shifted in his seat, looking as if he'd like to leave the room, too. "How are things going?" he asked cautiously, as if he knew the answer to the question.

Meadow said, "Horribly! I suppose Goldie must have told you about poor Devlin Wilson. The very *idea* of someone killing him in his own yard and in broad daylight! I simply can't believe it. Beatrice and I were at a guild meeting when it happened. Where were you?"

Beatrice hid a smile. There was no beating around the bush with Meadow. She always managed to come right to the point.

Gene flushed. "Well, I wasn't killing him, if that's what you're getting at. I always liked Devlin. He was a sort of simple guy and wasn't exactly an academic, but . . ." His voice trailed off as if he'd forgotten what his original point was. "He was always kind to me," he finished finally, picking up on the thread of his thought. "Anyway, I wouldn't have done it."

Meadow said, "I suppose you gave Ramsay a good alibi and everything?"

Gene was now frowning in annoyance. "As it happens, I was out and about yesterday . . . like yourself, it sounds."

"Liesss," hissed Miss Sissy.

Gene glanced sideways at her with alarm.

Beatrice asked, "Do you have any thoughts on who could have done something like this to Devlin? I didn't know him very well, but from what you're saying, it sounds like he was a nice guy who shouldn't have had a lot of enemies."

Gene opened his mouth and then closed it again with a hasty look in the direction of the back room. "Well, I meant that *I* didn't ever really have any issues with him. Not that everyone else didn't."

Meadow put her hands on her hips. "What on earth are you prattling about? Devlin was fantastic and everyone did like him."

Miss Sissy snorted at this as if it were obvious that murder victims are disliked by someone.

Gene looked cross at being interrupted. "Maybe you didn't know the real Devlin. He spread rumors around town. That's the kind of thing that makes folks in a small town furious. No one wants the whole town to know their business."

Meadow's brows were drawn together fiercely. "You're talking about Devlin *Wilson*? Are we speaking of the same person? I doubt it."

"Wickedness!" judged Miss Sissy.

"Anyway," continued Gene stiffly as Goldie walked back in with an apologetic smile for having stepped out, "I think there was another side to Devlin, that's all. I think there'd be plenty of people who'd have wanted him dead."

Goldie's eyes widened. "What on earth did I miss? I had no idea that Devlin had some sort of dark side."

"Total nonsense," said Meadow.

"Poppycock!" spat Miss Sissy as Meadow's Greek chorus.

Beatrice said, "Gene was just telling us that Devlin had plenty of people who might have wanted to murder him because of the fact he spread rumors in town."

Goldie's mouth dropped open and then she snapped it shut and gave a short laugh. "I think I know what's going on," she mused. She looked directly at Gene. "You're trying to protect me, aren't you?"

Miss Sissy made a disapproving clicking noise with her tongue.

Gene flushed and stuttered out, "I don't know what you mean."

Goldie said, "Only that you're trying to be nice. And I appreciate it." She turned to Beatrice and Meadow. "The fact is, Gene happened to see me leaving Devlin's house."

Meadow frowned until her entire face scrunched up. "But we *know* you were at Devlin's house. We saw you there. And you discovered Devlin's body. It wasn't exactly a secret, was it?"

Goldie said, "Yes, but what I didn't mention before is that's the *second* time I was there. You see, the first time I was there, I knocked on Devlin's door and just left, figuring he couldn't come to the door for some reason. But then I came by later because it was on my way home, his car was still in the driveway, and he was on my mind. That's when I became a little more concerned when he didn't answer the door. It wasn't like him to avoid speaking to me. The second time is when I discovered him."

Gene was looking even more uncomfortable and awkward than he had before.

Beatrice said, "So Gene, you *were* at Devlin's house, if you saw Goldie leave."

Goldie winced. "Sorry, Gene. I guess I sort of threw you under the bus there in the process of explaining my multiple trips. I *did* mention all this to Ramsay, but it's kind of a convoluted story and so I didn't get into all the twists and turns when I spoke with the two of you."

Beatrice said, "Actually, we'd already heard that Gene had been at Devlin's house from someone else. So you haven't incriminated him."

Gene scowled at Beatrice. "Who told you that I was there? Wait, let me guess. It must be Arnold Tremont again. Those folks cause no end of trouble. The question is, what was *Arnold* doing there when I arrived? I suspect he was there to silence Devlin before Devlin could tell everyone that he had evidence that Arnold killed Annabelle."

Meadow said, "That's not why he said he was there."

"Who even cares what he said? You know it's going to be a lie to cover up his involvement. He's determined to make me look like the guilty party and it's simply not true. I was unhappy with Annabelle, yes. I didn't lay a finger on her, though, and certainly wouldn't have murdered Devlin, whom I rather liked," Gene said stiffly.

Miss Sissy intoned, "Evillll."

Gene stared at her again and then shrugged. "Or, if you like, there's another possible solution. That Devlin murdered Annabelle because she wouldn't resume their relationship. I tell you, Devlin was absolutely obsessed with Annabelle."

Meadow said in surprise, "I didn't realize that you and Devlin were such good friends."

"I wouldn't call us *good friends*, but we did spend some time together, naturally, this being such a small town. But it wouldn't have taken a genius to realize that Devlin was completely besotted. When he and Annabelle started going out, I'd notice Devlin hanging out across the street like a lovelorn teenager. Then they were out on the town together, eating out. Devlin would always be holding Annabelle's hand or putting his arm around her as they walked down the street," said Gene with a shrug.

Beatrice said, "Then it seems odd that Devlin would murder her, since he was so in love with her."

A bit of pink rose up Gene's neck from his collar. "Maybe he struck out at her in frustration when she wouldn't return his affections. Or maybe he was furious at being dumped. Devlin killed her and Arnold somehow found out about it—I've heard he was in town when Annabelle died. Maybe he came home and realized later there was a clue that pointed to Devlin. Then Arnold, as the still-devoted husband, got his revenge by killing Devlin."

Meadow blinked at him. "I simply can't see Devlin killing someone."

"It's a possible solution," said Gene with great determination.

Goldie's phone rang again. She rolled her eyes. "Please excuse me. I don't usually get but a few calls a day and here I am getting them all at once. I'm starting to wonder if I can even fit in the manicure I'm supposed to be getting today." She took the call, stepping into the other room again.

As soon as the door closed behind her, Gene looked at Beatrice and Meadow urgently, almost a feverish glow about him. "Look, I know it doesn't look good, but Goldie would *never* have done something like this. Just look at her!" He waved his hands in the air as if to say that Goldie was at the pinnacle of some sort of tower of goodness and fortitude.

"You seem very keen on disproving her guilt," said Beatrice gently.

Gene slumped in his chair. "I couldn't stand it if Goldie went to jail. I just couldn't."

Beatrice said with dawning realization, "You think that she might have actually done it."

Gene quickly said, "Absolutely not. Only that it *appears* as though she might have done it. I'm just highlighting some other, very plausible, options."

Miss Sissy growled at him.

"Of *course* Goldie had nothing to do with it. How on earth *could* she? It's *Goldie*." Meadow sounded absolutely appalled and infuriated that anyone, her police chief husband included, could possibly think Goldie was involved.

Gene smiled gratefully at her. "Thank you. I don't think anyone could believe it, either."

Beatrice glanced at her watch and said, "Sorry, but we'll have to run for now. Meadow and I are taking Miss Sissy to the dentist."

Miss Sissy suddenly looked very glum as if she'd completely forgotten about the original errand in the excitement of speaking with Gene and Goldie.

Meadow said, "Should we all go in my van? I can drive back later to drop you off by your car, Beatrice."

"That's perfect."

And it was, although the van made a tremendous amount of noise on the way over to the dentist's office.

When they walked in, they found the office was quite busy; busy enough that they couldn't find three seats together. Meadow tried to sit next to Miss Sissy, but the old woman stomped across the waiting room to find a seat by herself, glaring at Meadow and Beatrice as if it was their fault that she was in this situation to begin with.

It was too loud in the waiting room for Beatrice and Meadow to even talk. A TV was going at full volume in one corner of the room and people in the waiting room were either listening to it or trying to talk over it, creating quite an uproar. Beatrice never understood why there were televisions in medical facilities. They only seemed to make her more on edge. Fortunately, the last time she'd been in a loud waiting room while waiting for her physical, she'd vowed to put her headphones in her purse for the following time. She fished around her bag and found them. Then she connected them to her phone and pulled up some relaxing music to listen to.

Meadow was reading food magazines and taking pictures of the most appealing recipes. Miss Sissy had fallen completely asleep, presumably snoring, although it couldn't be heard over the noise coming from the TV. Beatrice reflected that Miss Sissy's ability was a true gift, being able to fall asleep through the cacophony in that waiting room.

The room became a bit emptier as more people were taken back. Miss Sissy must truly have been worked in because they were there longer than patients who'd come in after they had. Finally, Miss Sissy's name was called.

"Do you want us to go back with you, Miss Sissy?" asked Meadow kindly.

Miss Sissy scowled at her and plodded off after the hygienist with a resigned sigh.

"Guess not," said Meadow with a shrug. She looked at Beatrice. "There's no one really in here now. Why don't we just turn the television down so we can talk?"

Beatrice unplugged her ears, glancing around the room. "An excellent idea!" She stood up and walked over to the TV, reaching up to turn the volume down. She smiled in relief as the screaming car dealership commercial turned into a whisper.

As she sat back down next to Meadow, Meadow demanded, "Now what do you make of everything we've heard? I'm sure you've got your opinions."

Beatrice said, "Let me hear what you're thinking, first."

Meadow shrugged. "I just think that none of them could have done it! I want it to be an outsider like Annabelle's husband, but every time I see Arnold I just like him too much to think that he could have done something like this. And he seemed to care for his wife too much to do it. So now I really want to hear what *you* have to say."

Beatrice said, "I think that we've seen that people who are under stress can act differently than they usually do. They think differently and they act differently. And all of these folks are under stress."

Meadow thought about this for a minute. "So Trixie is under stress because her husband was having an affair with Annabelle."

"Right. And when she found out about it, she made a clear ultimatum. It wasn't okay with her. She confronted her husband. Elias decided to stop seeing Annabelle. What we don't know is if Trixie *also* confronted Annabelle and what that confrontation might have looked like," said Beatrice.

Meadow snorted. "I can only imagine what that confrontation would have looked like. I don't think Trixie is some delicate flower who would have held back."

"That's what we don't know. After all, at least from her own accounts she showed a lot of restraint when she was telling Elias that he had to choose between Annabelle or herself. Maybe she showed similar restraint with Annabelle," said Beatrice.

Meadow snapped her fingers. "I *did* have something to tell you and I totally forgot about it. Ramsay finally came in last night, extremely late. Or was it really early?" She frowned.

"At any rate, it sounds as if it was dark outside," said Beatrice, in summary. She repressed a sigh. Meadow never believed in just giving the headlines of a story.

"Right. Anyway, I asked him how his case was going. Sometimes he just grumbles and says something about not being able to talk about investigations. But sometimes he actually gives us something valuable. It's a pity he can't be more consistent," said Meadow in exasperation.

"And what was it that he told you?" asked Beatrice, leading her on. At this rate, Miss Sissy would be back out with her fillings.

"Ramsay said that they'd checked out Annabelle's phone and that she'd made a whole bunch of calls to Elias," said Meadow, eyes wide.

Beatrice said, "So they were still speaking? This was during the period leading up to her death?"

"No, he said that Annabelle was making the calls, but Elias wasn't picking up. He also wasn't responding to all the text messages she was sending," said Meadow.

"And who knows? Maybe Annabelle even dropped by his house to see him if he wasn't responding to her on the phone," said Beatrice.

"Right! It sounded like Annabelle wasn't ready for the relationship to be over with," said Meadow.

"Or that *she* wanted to be the one to dump *him*, instead of the other way around," said Beatrice.

Meadow continued on with the suspects. "Going back to the suspects and stress levels. I guess Devlin was under a good deal of stress because he wanted to continue dating Annabelle and she dumped him."

"And then she died, causing a good deal of grief. And we all know how stressful grief can be," said Beatrice.

Meadow said, "But Devlin probably wasn't responsible for Annabelle's death, considering the fact that he's dead now."

"But he likely saw or heard something while he was in the area. Maybe it was something that he didn't fully understand, himself, until later on. Then the murderer realized that he was on to something and needed to be eliminated," said Beatrice.

"And then there's Gene," said Meadow. "Who is apparently completely gaga over Goldie. Why on earth was he over at Devlin's house? And we already know that he was under a lot of stress for quite a while. First, he fought having Annabelle's house built and then, he was trying to prevent the cell phone tower from being constructed."

"Exactly. And he doesn't have alibis for either one," said Beatrice with a shrug. "Who knows what he might have done if he had engaged in an argument in person with Annabelle? Maybe it just got out of hand. Maybe he only meant to scare her and things went too far."

Meadow said, "And Arnold Tremont. His major stress was the fact that he was about to be divorced by his wife when he wanted a reconciliation."

"Exactly. And I don't totally buy the fact that he was so completely friendly to his wife's boyfriends. I can't imagine him being so relaxed and laid-back about it," said Beatrice. "He's a man who built a successful business empire, and he did that by being pretty ruthless."

Meadow said, "So what's our next step?"

"My next step is to touch base again with Wyatt," said Beatrice. "And then I think you and I should do a little chatting at Annabelle's funeral."

Meadow snapped her fingers. "I totally forgot that there should be a funeral coming up!"

Beatrice said, "Wyatt was talking about the service some last night. He mentioned that Arnold is also hosting a reception."

Meadow blinked at her. "At his house? With all the boxes and everything in stacks on the floor?"

"No, he's renting out one of the downtown restaurants. I guess he wanted the Tremont family to offer an act of goodwill before leaving town. It might make the residents remember them more fondly," said Beatrice.

Chapter Twelve

Miss Sissy came back out into the waiting room, looking belligerent.

Beatrice muttered, "I wonder how that appointment went for the poor dentist. Miss Sissy looks as though she went in fighting."

Meadow said, "Almost makes you feel as though we should tip the poor woman." To Miss Sissy she said cheerfully, "All set to go?"

They made sure that Miss Sissy didn't need to check-out or make a follow-up appointment and then went on their way.

"Are you feeling any better?" asked Beatrice as they climbed into Meadow's van.

Miss Sissy muttered almost indistinguishably, "Can't feel tongue."

"Got it. Well then, I'm thinking you must be feeling better if you can't feel any pain," said Beatrice.

Meadow dropped Beatrice by her car and then headed off to take Miss Sissy home, her car making loud noises. While Beatrice was getting in her car, she saw Ramsay walking up on the sidewalk and raised a hand to wave.

"You just missed your wife," said Beatrice to Ramsay with a smile.

"A lucky escape," he said with a laugh. "I'm kidding—sort of. She's been a woman on a mission lately and when she's focused on something, she's not easy to live with."

Beatrice said, "At least what she's focused on is the same as you, right? Figuring out who's behind these crimes. Oh, and did you hear her car?"

"Don't tell me that you're also hallucinating the funny noises," said Ramsay, rolling his eyes. "Every time she insists that there's something wrong with the van, I check it to find it's working perfectly. And no, I didn't hear any noises as she left."

"Well, I can vouch for her that it's definitely there," said Beatrice with a chuckle. "She's not making it up. Maybe you should run it by a garage."

"What? And pay them three hundred dollars for the car to behave perfectly? No thank you. Meadow's van is far too crafty for that. But back to what we were talking about: figuring out the crimes. I'm curious to hear what you've found out," said Ramsay.

"Well, we just decided that people who are under stress react very differently than how they normally do," said Beatrice wryly.

Ramsay chuckled. "That sounds like the sort of thing you needed to say to calm Meadow down. She hates it when people she knows are duplicitous in any way."

Beatrice nodded. "It's tough when you've known people as long as Meadow has. These are folks she's grown up with, families that she's known different generations of. She has expectations that they'll follow a particular pattern of behavior. For me, it's a different story. I've only recently met everyone and I have the expectation that everyone in town has the ability to surprise me."

"What are your thoughts on the people connected with the case?" asked Ramsay, glancing around to make sure no one was in range to overhear them.

"Meadow and I did think that Gene was behaving sort of oddly."

"In what way?" asked Ramsay, looking innocent. He was obviously going to make her spell it out and work for any information that she received.

"Well, it sounded like he was almost *hanging out* at Devlin's house. At least, he was spotted there by Arnold Tremont," said Beatrice. "If his purpose wasn't to murder Devlin, I'm not sure what it was. And for him to be pulled over on the side of the road like that? It just seems like an odd thing to have done, that's all. It didn't sound as if he was visiting anyone on the street or that he had any architectural reasons to be there. He was very awkward the entire conversation."

"And he *should* have felt awkward," said Ramsay. He chuckled. "Apparently, he's been following Goldie around like a lovesick puppy. We had to pull that information out of him, of course. He's been very cagey about it. He definitely wins the prize for not being forthright."

"What? Like Gene is *stalking* Goldie?" asked Beatrice, making a face.

"I don't know if she'd call it stalking. If she did, I'd be sure to do something about it. That's the last problem we need to have in Dappled Hills. Goldie seems to be sort of touched by it, oddly," said Ramsay.

"By having Gene follow her around?" asked Beatrice.

"That's right. I guess it's not stalking if it has her blessing," said Ramsay with a shrug.

Beatrice said, "What did Gene say?"

"That he was on the scene because he'd been tailing Goldie in the hopes of serendipitously running into her," said Ramsay, rolling his eyes. "Apparently, he wasn't able to find a good excuse to speak with her and he wanted it to be natural. I felt like I was talking to someone who was romantically stunted. It was like having a conversation with a middle school boy."

Beatrice frowned. "But earlier he was sitting in her office with a bucket of fried chicken. That was hardly accidental."

Ramsay chuckled. "Well, he probably used the excuse that he'd heard she'd had a traumatic evening yesterday. That he wanted to bring her lunch to cheer her up."

"That certainly sounds likely," said Beatrice dryly. "All right, so to recap. He was following Goldie's car, I'm assuming at a discreet distance. Considering that most of Goldie's work involves downtown businesses, maybe Gene was hoping he could run into her at the pharmacy or Bub's Grocery, or the ice cream shop or somewhere. Goldie ran quickly by Devlin's house to ask him about something regarding downtown Dappled Hills. Devlin didn't answer the door."

Ramsay said, "Right. But remember, Devlin might not have been deceased at that time. He was likely simply working outside and didn't hear her. We don't have a very firm time for when he died."

"But the pavers were in the side yard. Devlin wouldn't have been able to miss her if she was standing there knocking at his door," said Beatrice with a frown.

"Devlin was something of an overachiever yesterday, apparently, and was also working in his *back* yard. Weeding and whatnot. What's more, he had earbuds in his ears and the music, when we found him, was cranked up way past the recommended decibel level," said Ramsay.

"So he might not have been able to hear someone approaching," said Beatrice slowly.

"Exactly. Nor might he have been paying attention at all."

Beatrice said with a sigh, "He'd alluded to the fact that this project of his was a way to keep himself distracted from thinking about Annabelle and her death. So you're right—he might have been totally absorbed in what he was doing."

"Even if he wasn't, he wouldn't have heard anything over that music," said Ramsay.

Beatrice continued, "So Goldie leaves, upon getting no response from Devlin. Gene tags along somewhere behind her in his car. While they're there, they see Arnold Tremont. At any rate, he sees *them*. He's trying to contact Devlin, allegedly to use him to sell the house. He receives no response."

Ramsay nods. "It's sort of like Grand Central Station over at Devlin's house."

"Then Goldie swings back by on her way back to the office. This time she spots Devlin in the side yard and thinks at first that he's just taking a nap. And Gene was apparently not still following her at this point?" asked Beatrice.

"That's right. Because he engineered another 'serendipitous' meeting at the previous location. They had a coffee together and it was mission accomplished for him," said Ramsay. He gave her a sideways glance. "By the way, you might be interested to know that the state police aren't considering you as a suspect at all."

Beatrice smiled. "That's good. Although I'd almost forgotten that I'd been considered a suspect in the first place. What made them come to that decision?"

"Just the fact that it didn't make any sense at all. Why would you commit murder over an ancient sword and then leave the sword at the scene of the crime? And then tell us about the connection between you and the sword when there was no way on God's green earth that we were going to find that on our own?"

Beatrice nodded. "I'd be a pretty lousy murderer, if that were the case."

Ramsay said, "And you clearly were at a guild meeting and then with Meadow during Devlin's murder, which then completely ruled you out." He gave a short laugh. "Now I just need to figure out who *else* to rule out so we can find who's behind these deaths." He rubbed his temples as if they hurt. "Well, I should be getting along. You take care, all right? I don't think Wyatt would be happy if anything happened to you."

Beatrice said, "I'll be careful. Thanks for the update!"

Beatrice stopped by the grocery store on the way back home. She'd gotten used to Bub's limited options, but imagined that Annabelle had not in the short time she'd been in Dappled Hills. Beatrice remembered when she'd first moved to town and found that there weren't any ready-to-eat meals in the deli section . . . or, actually, much of a deli section at all. She'd been widowed for a good number of years in Atlanta and after Piper had left for college, she'd gotten in the habit of not doing much cooking. Moving back to Dappled Hills had forced her to pick it back up.

But today when she went into the grocery store, she saw some new items. She lifted her eyebrows. Smoked salmon? Fancy crackers?"

Bert, who was one of the regular employees, saw her eyeing the smoked salmon. He barked out a laugh. "You look surprised to see that here."

"I'm stunned—and delighted! What fresh magic is this?" asked Beatrice, picking up a package and reading the label in wonder.

Bert said, "That rich lady was in here giving the boss an earful about not stocking stuff she liked. She said she wasn't used to having all the food she enjoyed when she lived in Atlanta. Then she wrote out a list of all the things she wanted to see in the store. For half a minute, I thought she was going to buy the place to have it exactly the way she wanted it."

Beatrice nodded. "So this is all Annabelle Tremont's doings. If we all purchase these things, does that mean that you'll continue stocking them?"

Bert said, "Sure. Whatever sells, you know. Boss just didn't want to take a risk earlier, stocking stuff and then nobody buying it."

Beatrice made a point to walk through the entire store (considering its size, this was an easy task) and purchasing anything that she recognized as being new or even vaguely exotic. She might not have been a friend of Annabelle's, but she had to admit that she had some good ideas. No wonder Goldie had decided to try to partner with her in her efforts to improve the town.

When she got home, she saw that she'd beaten Wyatt back from the church. Beatrice decided to set up a whole smorgasbord for supper. She lightly cooked the fresh asparagus she'd bought with some olive oil and Parmesan cheese, mixed quinoa with spinach and grape tomatoes, and laid out the smoked salmon and crackers.

Wyatt's eyes lit up when he walked through the door. "Do my eyes deceive me, or is that smoked salmon I see?"

"Yes, and you won't believe where I got it," said Beatrice.

"Did you drive to Asheville or Charlotte for it?" asked Wyatt, looking bemused as he gazed at the feast in front of him.

"Believe it or not, no. Bub's Grocery had it in stock," said Beatrice with a grin when Wyatt's face displayed shock and disbelief.

"*Our* Bub's?" he asked, as if there were a chain of Bub's Groceries that contained much better selections than their own.

"That's right. Apparently, Annabelle had been going over there and complaining about the food that was kept in stock. That resulted in some amazing options today. But we all have to buy them so they'll continue to stock them." Beatrice gestured for Wyatt to sit down and he did.

Wyatt blessed the meal and then they started eating. Beatrice closed her eyes after taking a bite of the salmon. "I could get used to this. Although it's not in the budget for us to eat smoked salmon every day."

"We could," said Wyatt lightly. "Then we'd be the most chichi grandparents around."

Beatrice grinned at him. "Somehow, I can't quite picture that. Although I can quite easily picture us as grandparents."

"How do you picture us?" asked Wyatt.

Beatrice finished a bite of her asparagus. "I see you sitting on the sofa and reading a story to the grandbaby. And he or she is totally enthralled. And I can see me playing a game with the baby . . . maybe Memory . . . and losing badly."

Wyatt said, "I never was good at Memory, even when I was a kid. I was always sure I remembered where the matching butterfly tile was, and being completely wrong."

Beatrice laughed and they ate for a few moments in a comfortable silence.

Then Wyatt asked, "How did things go today?"

Beatrice said, "It was an interesting day. Meadow is bound and determined for us to figure out who did it . . . yesterday. So we didn't spare any time on that mission. We talked to people all day."

Wyatt said, "Sounds like a busy day."

"It was. And to top it all off, we even managed to take Miss Sissy to the dentist to see about a toothache," said Beatrice. "That was apparently the mysterious reason that she had you come over on Sunday afternoon. If she'd just told you what was wrong, we could have gotten her to a dentist yesterday. Instead, she put it off, and she was pretty uncomfortable today."

Wyatt groaned. "There's nothing worse than a toothache. I guess maybe she was in denial about it or just hoping it would go away on its own."

"That's the thing about teeth. The toothache never seems to get *better* until you do something about it," said Beatrice. "Anyway, that's the recap of our day."

Wyatt grinned at her. "Now I feel as though my day was less-productive. All I managed to do was to sit in on the prayer breakfast, draw up a draft for the sermon, and then visit a few folks at the retirement home."

"Sounds plenty busy to me," said Beatrice.

They finished up their meal and then cleaned up together with Noo-noo hovering closely nearby, hoping for a few scraps. But it had been such a good meal, eclectic though it was, that there wasn't anything left over. Beatrice filled one of the corgi's rubber Kongs with kibbles and peanut butter and the little dog worked on it for the next hour while Wyatt read *David Copperfield* and Beatrice pulled out the fabric from the brown paper bag. She frowned at it, trying to picture it as something other than just a flat piece of brown fabric with birds perched on green vines. She knew she didn't have time for a quilt before December, not in addition to the one she was already working on. A pillow? The problem with making a pillow out of the fabric was that it might not match or even complement the other colors in the quilter's room. The last thing she wanted was to make the project stand out like a sore thumb.

Wyatt said, "You know, this book has really grown on me. At first I think I wasn't just completely invested in the character, but he's such a cheerful little guy, when all this terrible stuff is happening to him. And Mr. Micawber is *wonderful*."

Beatrice grunted at him absently and then, realizing she hadn't really been listening, said, "Sorry. I guess I'm caught up in my own head right now."

"Something wrong?" Wyatt asked.

"Oh, it's the paper bag project thing. I'm trying to figure out what to make with it so that it will be a decent Christmas present for a guild member," said Beatrice.

Wyatt said, "You told me that you'd found out what it was, but you didn't tell *me* what it was."

"Sorry," Beatrice said again. "I've been so absentminded with these deaths that I feel like I'm walking around in a cloud. It was pretty basic—it's sort of like a secret Santa. Everyone put some fabric in a brown bag, Posy keeps track of who has what, and the quilter who opens the bag has to make something while using the fabric."

"And gives it to the quilter as a Christmas present?" asked Wyatt.

"That's right."

Wyatt said, "But Christmas is months away. You don't have to worry about the fabric tonight, do you?"

"I *don't*, but the problem is that it takes me a while to set everything up. For one thing, I don't even know what to make with this fabric. It doesn't have to be a quilt," said Beatrice. She glared at the fabric as if it was its fault for being particularly difficult and uninspiring.

Wyatt considered the fabric. "Couldn't you always do something small, like a potholder or something?"

Beatrice said, "I definitely could and it would save me a lot of time and hassle. I'm working on a quilt already—the one that's a bookshelf pattern with lots of different titles in different fabrics. I thought I might give it to Piper as a Christmas present since she's always enjoyed reading so much. Although I also picked up a really cute fabric at Posy's for the baby."

"Maybe a smaller project would work better, then, if you're working on two things at once. The bookshelf pattern sounds great and Piper will probably love getting something of her own that's not for the baby," said Wyatt gently.

Beatrice brightened. "That's true. The problem is that I don't want to be the only one bringing in potholders when other members are bringing in quilts. I want to do something cute with it." She tilted her head to one side. "Or maybe make something useful with it."

"Tote bag?" asked Wyatt. "It seems like that would be useful for a quilter. I know you're always carrying a bunch of stuff back and forth from guild meetings and shows."

Beatrice nodded, looking at the fabric. "You know, I can actually see this as a tote bag. And it would be useful and cute at the same time." She got up and gave Wyatt a hug. "Thanks. And I'm glad you're enjoying *David Copperfield*, by the way. I don't think I even answered you back before."

"It was an inspired recommendation," he said, pulling her in close.

The next morning, Wyatt was reading over his notes for Annabelle's funeral while Beatrice made them a pot of black coffee. They'd both woken up a little groggy from a hard sleep, but the pot she made was definitely overkill. The coffee was so strong that both of them had to choke it down, despite loading it up with cream and sugar.

"That coffee is practically a solid," said Beatrice, making a face. "Now I'm not sure that I even have an appetite for breakfast. I just ate six ounces of coffee."

"We should probably make a stab at it, although I'm not starving, myself. It's going to be a long time until we have the chance to eat again," said Wyatt.

Beatrice said, "Remind me again what the plan is for after the service?"

"Reception honoring Annabelle at The Willows restaurant downtown," said Wyatt automatically. He glanced at the clock. "Don't you want to attend the service with Meadow? You'll be there too early if you go with me."

Beatrice said, "I forgot to tell you that she texted me last night right before I was going to bed. She'd forgotten that she had something she had to do right before the service, so would have to go straight there. It's fine—I don't mind being there early."

Chapter Thirteen

An hour later, they were at the cemetery for the graveside service. The sun was shining, but fortunately the section of the cemetery they were in was a heavily shaded one. It was a beautiful old cemetery with roads that wound through the grounds by ancient graves. Old oaks created a lovely canopy for the mourners below. Arnold was there when they arrived, despite the fact they were early, but then, he'd always been as hyper-punctual as Annabelle had been.

Beatrice walked up to him. Arnold's face was serious, and he reached out to give her a hug as if he'd needed one. Beatrice gave him a squeeze in return. "I'm so sorry, Arnold. I know how much you cared about Annabelle."

He nodded, momentarily choked up. "Thanks for that, Beatrice. I'm glad you're here."

He and Wyatt went over the arrangements one last time and Beatrice walked away to leave them to it as other people arrived. Apparently, Arnold had asked Wyatt for names of choir members and musicians the church used for special musical services at Christmas and Easter. A florist was there also, putting the finishing touches on some elaborate arrangements. These were nothing like the usual sprays that were at most of the services Beatrice had attended. One had daylilies in rusty oranges with trailing ivy and other seasonal foliage that Beatrice couldn't identify.

Beatrice watched from a nearby bench as a soloist arrived along with several musicians bearing wind instruments and books of music. A light breeze kept her cool.

A few minutes later, cars started pulling up. Beatrice was curious to see if Annabelle's family would be there. Annabelle had been such a private person that she didn't even know if she had much family at all. Instead, all she saw were people from Dappled Hills. It was a full fifteen minutes before she saw a couple that she'd been acquainted with in the arts community in Atlanta. The husband gave her a quick smile as he spotted her and Beatrice walked over to talk briefly to them. As she'd suspected, they were there to support Arnold and hadn't been particularly close to Annabelle.

"Are you going to the reception afterward?" asked Beatrice.

The wife shook her head. "No, we're actually on our way to Georgia, but took a little detour to pay our respects to Arnold. We'll be leaving right after the service."

The husband looked curiously at Beatrice. "So you're living here full-time now? How do you like it? Somehow, I've always pictured you at an urban museum. This is such a beautiful little town, but I'm sure it likely doesn't house a major art museum.

"I've retired, actually. And that's what retirement is all about . . . doing something different," said Beatrice with a smile. "It's been a nice change of pace here."

They chatted for a few more minutes. When she'd sat back down on her bench again, Goldie, who'd just arrived at the cemetery, walked over to her. "It seems like too pretty of a day to have a funeral," she said with a sigh.

Beatrice said, "Isn't it? Usually it's horribly hot or pouring down rain."

"Although Annabelle's husband made the cemetery as beautiful as I've ever seen it. Those flowers are incredible and I love the chamber music that's playing." Goldie sat quietly for a few moments and said, "It's just a terrible shame, isn't it? It wasn't Annabelle's time to go. The more I think about it, the worse I feel. She had so many years ahead of her and she was obviously excited about starting out in Dappled Hills."

Beatrice thought wryly that Goldie was likely transferring her own love of Dappled Hills to Annabelle. She said carefully, "I think she was excited for a fresh start, yes. It's sad that it didn't work out."

"Oh, I know that she wanted some changes in town. But she was looking out for us, wasn't she? She wanted the town to focus on getting even better!" Goldie's eyes shone.

Beatrice said, "As a matter of fact, I saw the result of some of Annabelle's activism in town just yesterday at Bub's Grocery. There was smoked salmon in there and a variety of foods that I'd never seen before. I'm trying to spread the news so that everyone buys it out and gets it restocked."

"That's exactly what I'm saying," said Goldie. "She wanted to make a difference. I feel like her end-game was to have Dappled Hills be a real *destination*. A resort town. And instead, of being able to implement all the changes that she dreamed about, she was struck down in her prime. What an awful way to go, too—being stabbed with a sword!" She shuddered.

Beatrice suddenly sat very still and looked at Goldie appraisingly. Trixie had called Goldie a girl scout and Beatrice couldn't disagree. Goldie was the type of person who tried to see the good in people and usually succeeded. She was the type of person who tried to effect positive changes in town and pull everyone together to make Dappled Hills better. Could she also be the type of person who is so passionate about her causes that she strikes out impetuously and kills?

Beatrice took a deep breath. "Goldie, how did you know that Annabelle was murdered with a sword?"

Goldie's brow wrinkled. "What do you mean? Isn't that how she died? You were there, so you know, don't you? You'd have seen it."

"Yes, but the way she died was not released to the public. The police wanted that kept quiet and so the few of us that were privy to the information have been very careful not to say anything about it," said Beatrice.

Goldie suddenly seemed agitated, picking nervously at her fingernails. "I don't know, Beatrice. I'm not sure where I heard that. You know how many people that I talk to in a day. All I do is drive around or walk around town and talk to business owners and residents. I could have heard about the sword anywhere." She gazed anxiously at Beatrice as if she'd really like to help her but wasn't exactly sure how.

One of the musicians started playing a hymn a bit louder than the chamber music had been. This was apparently the cue that the service was about to start. Goldie looked relieved. "It looks like it's time for the service." She hesitated as if not sure what to say next. "Um, sorry, Beatrice."

Beatrice slowly walked over to stand at the back of the mourners. How could Goldie have heard that information if she weren't the person responsible for murdering Annabelle?

She saw out of the corner of her eye that Meadow's van had pulled up in a rush. Equally in a rush, Meadow hurried out of her car, smoothing her dress as she went. She caught Beatrice's eye and made a face at her lateness. A minute later, she sidled up to Beatrice.

The service was one of the nicest ones that Beatrice had ever been to. The instruments sounded beautiful in the quiet setting. The steady breeze and shade kept the temperatures down. And the soloist's rendition of "Abide With Me" made chills go up Beatrice's spine.

Wyatt, who was frequently in the position of having to speak about someone he didn't know very well, did an excellent job with the background information that both Beatrice and Arnold had provided him.

When the service was over, everyone filed over to speak with Arnold. He apparently told all the gathered to be sure to attend the reception at The Willows in downtown Dappled Hills. No one needed to be told twice since it was one of the best eateries in town. Inside the white-tablecloth restaurant, the owner himself had set out buffet tables topped with chafing dishes full of prime rib, three-cheese pasta, garlic mashed potatoes, and chicken medallions with sweet potato wedges.

"I may never eat again," murmured Beatrice to Wyatt. They were to be sitting with Arnold since Wyatt had officiated at the

service, and the owner had carefully laid out name cards to indicate this at one of the tables. However, Arnold didn't appear
to be in the position to be able to sit or eat anything anytime
soon. The town of Dappled Hills, after being given such fine
treatment, was determined to speak with Arnold and pay their
respects.

Meadow breathlessly joined them in the line. "I know you're
both sitting with Arnold, but would you mind if I joined you if
there's room at the table?"

Wyatt said, "I'm sure there is—I think there are several
more chairs there."

Meadow made a face. "Just as long as Ramsay isn't joining
us. He's spent the entire morning staring at people suspiciously."

Beatrice laughed as they walked over to their table. "That's
his job, after all. I doubt the poor man will even sit down or have
a bite to eat. When I saw him at the service, he was hovering at
the back and keeping an eye on everyone. He's simply trying to
figure out who's responsible and if they're here today."

Meadow snorted. "Well, of *course* they're here."

Wyatt frowned. "Do you know something we don't?"

"Only that the entire *town* is here practically. The good citi-
zens of Dappled Hills wouldn't have wanted to miss out on this!
Even weddings here aren't this elaborate," said Meadow.

Beatrice agreed. Arnold must have hired a small army and
spent a fortune to get this set up in time. Not only had he
hired out the most expensive restaurant in town, but he'd hired
a florist to fill the restaurant with flowers. Magnolia blossoms
floated in bowls on the tables and there were large floral arrangements everywhere in riotous color. Not only that, but the musi-

cians from the funeral had come over and were now softly playing a selection by Ravel.

Arnold was still engaged in conversation with guests and motioned to them with a small smile to start eating and not let their food get cold.

Beatrice said to Meadow in a low voice as she picked up her fork, "Did you tell anyone about the sword?"

"What? No! Don't even mention such a thing. Ramsay would absolutely have my head if I spilled one of the most important details from the murder scene." Meadow clutched her neck as if making sure her head was still attached to it. "What makes you ask that?"

"Because Goldie Parsons mentioned it in passing at the service," said Beatrice with a sigh. She took a big bite of garlic mashed potatoes. It was delicious and the perfect comfort food. Still, she figured she wouldn't even want supper after eating all of this food.

"*Goldie* did?" asked Meadow, sounding outraged. "How on earth could she know about that? The only people who knew were Ramsay, the state police, Wyatt, me and you."

Wyatt lifted his hands up. "Believe me, I haven't said a word."

Beatrice said, "No, you're always excellent at keeping secrets. And I haven't let anything slip. We know Ramsay wouldn't. I figured you might be the weak link, Meadow."

Meadow said earnestly, "Ordinarily, I might agree with you. Oh, you know, if it were something innocuous like someone is dating someone else or a surprise birthday party. *That* kind of secret I find hard to keep. But I would *never* have said anything about this. It would possibly mess up our chances at finding out who did this."

Wyatt said slowly, "Then, if it wasn't any of us, it could only have been—"

"The killer," finished Beatrice.

Meadow turned her head and quite obviously scanned the room. She spotted Goldie chatting with Gene, surrounded by a group of people who all seemed to be having a good time while trying very hard to remember and behave like they were at a funeral reception. "Unbelievable," she muttered.

Beatrice said, "Now remember, we don't know that this proves that *Goldie* is the killer. All it proves is that she knew about the weapon."

Wyatt said, "Right. Someone else could have told her about it."

"But *that* person was probably the killer," said Meadow. "So who told her about it? Did you ask her?"

Beatrice said, "I did. I felt sort of bad at pressing her at the funeral, but I needed to know. The problem was that she couldn't remember who'd told her."

Meadow frowned. "Is she trying to protect someone by keeping that info quiet?" Then she gasped, putting her hand to her mouth. "Gene! Maybe Gene told her and she's trying to cover up for him."

Beatrice said, "Honestly, it seemed more like she couldn't remember."

Meadow said, "But how could you forget something like that? That's unbelievable. I'd definitely remember who'd given me a piece of information about a crime scene."

Wyatt said reasonably, "I would, too. But we can't forget that Goldie talks to many more people in a day than we do. Almost all of her day is spent speaking with business owners and other people."

"That's true," said Meadow slumping.

"Plus, who knows if she heard it from the killer directly? Perhaps the killer let something slip days ago and then that person told someone else and then it progressed from there," said Beatrice.

Meadow sighed. "I suppose we *are* in Dappled Hills. That's a distinct possibility. So it's completely fruitless."

Beatrice said, "I don't think so. I'd like to talk to the person that Goldie heard it from first and then proceed from there. It might really be a lead."

Meadow said darkly, "I'd prefer to think of it as a lead. Otherwise, I'm going to get far too down about all this."

Wyatt said mildly, "Maybe we should change the subject, then. Speak of other things." He glanced up and said, "It looks like Georgia is heading over."

Meadow suddenly looked more cheerful. "Oh good. I wanted to see how she's doing."

"Has Georgia been having a rough stretch lately?" asked Wyatt, looking concerned.

Beatrice nodded. "I can't believe that I haven't mentioned that. It just goes to show how crazy things have been lately. But yes."

"Maybe you and I should plan a short visit sometime in the future?" asked Wyatt. "Maybe with some cupcakes from June Bug?"

Beatrice smiled at him. She loved this man with his common sense and his concern for others. "That sounds perfect. Maybe one day right after school when the students have already left for the day."

Georgia walked up to their table and smiled shyly at them. Beatrice was relieved to see that she was looking a little less anxious than the last time she'd seen her.

"Hi Georgia," the three of them chorused together as Meadow leapt up to give Georgia a quick hug.

"How are things going?" asked Beatrice.

Georgia said, "Good! I actually took a personal day today at school, which I haven't done in years. I fit in a dental appointment first thing this morning, then ran a few errands that I'd had no time to do. Then I thought I'd attend the service today, too."

"Well, we're glad to see you," said Wyatt with a grin.

"Have you gotten your nails done yet?" asked Meadow, craning to see Georgia's fingernails.

Georgia shook her head. "I'm going soon, I promise. I ran by there after school, but Trixie had already gone for the day and the other lady had appointments. I'll try again soon. But I wanted to tell you the best news."

Beatrice opened her eyes wide. "Tony got a job?"

Georgia's smile widened until it engulfed her entire face. "He did!"

Now they were all giving Georgia a hug.

"That's fantastic news!" said Beatrice.

"Isn't it? And his benefits are great, too. He's already given notice at the hardware store," said Georgia. "And I won't have to find a second job anymore!"

Meadow beamed at her. "You must be so relieved."

"You just don't know," said Georgia with a sigh. "It's been a lot of stress to start a marriage on. For one thing, I felt like we never really saw each other. I was at school, he was at the hardware store and then in class. It was almost like we were suddenly living separate lives, which neither of us wanted."

"But you got through it just fine," said Beatrice.

Georgia said, "I just wanted to catch y'all up and thank you for being so supportive. I don't know what I'd have done if I'd had to just absorb all of my worries and not talk about them. Thanks for being here."

Meadow, predictably, misted up. "We'll *always* be here. Don't you worry about that."

"And you're not only here for me, but my sister, too. Savannah called me last night and sounded so pleased. She absolutely *loved* visiting the retirement community last night," said Georgia.

Wyatt said, "Oh good. We were hoping that would be a good fit for her. And it means a lot to some of our folks who can't get out as much there."

Georgia nodded. "I think she was especially excited because she won a Scrabble game and a game of checkers! You know how Savannah can be. She's looking forward to her next visit there. It's so good for her to stay busy."

Wyatt said, "Well, we're good at keeping volunteers busy! We also have a group that goes over to the retirement communities to help with communion and holiday events. I'll talk with her later to see if she'd be interested in those service opportunities, too."

Georgia smiled at them. "I have the feeling that would be a yes. Okay, well, I should let y'all finish your food now. It was good talking to you. And thanks to you both."

Georgia walked to her table as Meadow frowned as she looked toward Arnold. "Someone should really rescue that man. He's been standing for a long time and hasn't had a bite to eat."

Beatrice said, "Oh, I think Arnold Tremont wouldn't have a problem in the world breaking away from anyone that he didn't want to talk to."

"He may not have much of an appetite," said Wyatt. "Sometimes grief can hit a person that way."

Meadow clucked. "He still needs to eat. And people should respect that. What on earth are they thinking?"

Before they knew what Meadow had in mind, she hopped out of her chair and strode over to where Arnold was standing with a small group of people. Beatrice had to admit that he did look tired. At the very least, he should have a glass of water.

Wyatt winked at Beatrice as Meadow appeared briefly to tell the people speaking with Arnold that it was time for Arnold to eat some food. The people quickly dissipated as Meadow practically dragged Arnold back to the table with them.

Chapter Fourteen

As Arnold sat down, Meadow said, slightly out of breath, "Now let me get you a plate or else you'll attract a swarm of people again. Residents tend to attack new people."

Arnold opened his mouth to thank her, but she was already stomping over to the buffet line, appearing to be prepared to push people out of her way if they attempted to get in between her and the food.

Arnold gave a small laugh. His eyes were tired. "Everyone has been very nice. I don't understand why Annabelle was having a hard time here. They certainly are friendly."

Beatrice asked, "Did Annabelle say she wasn't enjoying living here?" She kept an eye on Meadow. The last thing they needed was Meadow coming back to the table and ardently defending Dappled Hills.

Arnold sighed. "Not outright. But she didn't sound as happy as she should have, either. But Annabelle was like that. She'd set off for something she wanted, determined to get it and to fight for it. Then she'd get it and the thrill of competition was over and she wasn't as interested anymore."

"Is that what you think happened here?" asked Wyatt.

Arnold said, "In some ways. Also, honestly, the friendliness of the residents might have been an issue for her, too. She did value her privacy and wasn't used to casual conversation around town. But besides that, I think part of her really relished her struggle to get the house she wanted. She liked sparring with Gene over the property and the house she wanted built. Then, when the house was finally available to her, she wasn't quite as interested in it anymore."

Beatrice said, "Annabelle also seemed to be trying to make changes in the town. She was at town hall meetings fighting for a new cell tower."

Arnold smiled reminiscently. "That was my girl. Yes, she complained about the reception here when she was on the phone with me. We had a lot of dropped calls and then sometimes I couldn't get through to her line at all and had to leave a message."

Beatrice said with a smile, "There is also evidence that she was making inroads into the selection of foods at Bub's Market, down the road."

Arnold nodded. "She'd mentioned the fact that there weren't any really high-quality options there. Once she'd gotten her way, she wouldn't have cared as much." He paused. "And it was even the same with the guys she was seeing. After the thrill of the chase was over, she never wanted to pursue the relationship any further."

Beatrice asked, "So it was natural what happened with Devlin? That she tired of it after they became an established couple?"

Arnold nodded. "In my experience, that's true."

"So, in reality, Trixie probably didn't need to issue her ultimatum to her husband because Annabelle's and Elias's relationship was doomed from the start," said Beatrice.

"That's right. It wouldn't have had a chance," said Arnold. "Annabelle would have gotten tired of it in another couple of weeks."

Wyatt said, "It sounds like that makes the relationship between the two of you even more special. It's lasted."

Arnold's eyes glistened, and he took a moment before he spoke. "Yes. I suppose we beat the odds there. Or almost did. Annabelle was planning on a divorce, as I've mentioned, but I was determined to change her mind."

Meadow returned with not one, but two plates of food. She laid them down in front of Arnold and said briskly, "I wasn't sure what you wanted, so I got you some of everything. I can attest to the fact that everything in this restaurant is top-notch."

Arnold smiled at her and Beatrice could see that driven element that had made him such a success. "I wouldn't have expected anything less."

An hour later, Wyatt and Beatrice were back home. They were so full from the reception that they both ended up taking naps. Beatrice woke up feeling groggy and a little unsettled. She felt as though there had been some information that she'd heard that day that she needed to sort through.

Wyatt stirred and woke up, giving her a smile as he stretched.

"How do you feel?" he asked with a yawn.

"Not great, honestly," said Beatrice. "I think I must have fallen right into a very deep sleep and now I feel groggy. Plus, I still have that over-full feeling from all the food I ate earlier. How about you?"

"I feel completely refreshed," said Wyatt in an apologetic voice. "In fact, I was thinking about going to my office and getting some things knocked out. Maybe get ahead on my sermons or something."

Beatrice said, "If you have that much energy, that sounds like a good idea. I'm thinking I should go for a walk. That might help me from feeling so sluggish and clear my head a little."

At the word *walk*, Noo-noo's ears perked up. She grinned her corgi grin at Beatrice, tilting her head to one side and wagging her tiny nubbin of a tail. Beatrice reached out and gave her a rub. "And you can come too, Noo-noo."

Wyatt hesitated. "Sure you don't want me to come with you?"

"Not unless you're dying for a walk for some reason. It sounds like you might end up being more productive doing work," said Beatrice.

Minutes later, Wyatt set off in the direction of the church, waving as Beatrice hopped into the car to take Noo-noo for a hike on a mountain trail instead of their usual stroll around the neighborhood. Beatrice felt as though she could use a few more hills in her walk today. And Noo-noo especially loved all the smells along the mountain trail.

Beatrice was so deep in her thoughts that she didn't notice when a car pulled up rather quickly in the small parking lot at the entrance of the trail. Nor did she notice a car door slam as she headed up the trail at a pace that Noo-noo's short legs had to work hard to match.

Finally, however, she did notice when a loud, breathless voice fussed, "Beatrice! Slow down!"

Beatrice spun around and sighed with relief to see a red-faced Meadow. "For heaven's sake! You scared me to death." Noo-noo trotted over to Meadow and nuzzled her leg.

Meadow gave her an exasperated snort as she reached down to love on Noo-noo. "I think you need to have your hearing checked. I called your name at a *very* high volume when I stepped out of my car. You didn't even turn around! If you were scared, it's your own fault."

Beatrice sighed. "Sorry. I'm just preoccupied. Thinking about these murders."

"Well, I am too, and that's why I followed you when I spotted your car driving toward the trail. I figured you were going for a walk and I decided I'd join you. I happened to have my walking shoes on." Meadow stuck out a foot to show a well-worn athletic shoe. "It's a good thing I wasn't the murderer, or you'd be dead by now."

They headed out on the trail and Meadow said curiously, "So what *are* you thinking that you're so absorbed?"

Beatrice said, "I really don't even know. I keep feeling as if there's something I'm missing. And after all the food from this morning, and a long nap, I felt like I needed to clear my head."

Meadow said in a pointed tone, "First of all, can we slow down just a hair? Some of us aren't quite as fit as others, you know."

Beatrice immediately slowed her pace and Meadow looked relieved. "Thank you. Besides, I couldn't keep up a conversation if I was panting from exertion. How about if I tell you what *I'm* thinking and you can tell me what you think. I can be Watson to your Sherlock."

"Sounds good. I feel pretty directionless right now." Beatrice stopped briefly for Noo-noo to sniff at a rhododendron. She glanced over at Meadow.

Meadow said fervently, "I'm thinking that we need to head over to Goldie's office tomorrow morning and confront her. I want to shake her until her teeth rattle!"

Beatrice chuckled. "You can't do that, Meadow. Just think what the town will say if the police chief's wife assaults the downtown developer. Then you really *will* have plenty of time to figure out how best to decorate the police station."

"I didn't say I wanted to *assault* Goldie. I just want to make her see sense," said Meadow, looking stormy. "Doesn't she realize that by withholding information from us that she might be allowing a really dangerous person to strike again?"

"I don't think she's deliberately withholding information. She seemed more as if she simply couldn't remember who she'd been talking to," said Beatrice mildly.

"Then maybe a little rattling around might make her remember," said Meadow. Then she said in a quieter voice, "Never mind me. I'm just getting very frustrated. There's a part of me that wonders if maybe Goldie is the killer, after all. Sometimes it's the person you'd least expect. And she's definitely the one that I wouldn't have picked in a million years as a killer. Still, I keep thinking about how upset she was at that meeting when Annabelle was belittling her."

"Let's pay her another visit tomorrow," said Beatrice. "I can ask her if she remembered anything. Maybe something will have occurred to her. I did sort of put her on the spot at the funeral service."

Meadow said, "Or maybe she's gone starry-eyed over Gene, although that's very difficult to imagine. She could think that somehow Gene is involved and be trying to cover for him. Gene could have told her about the sword, and then she realized she needed to conceal the fact."

"Maybe. Right now it's hard to say. We might be able to find out more when we talk to her tomorrow. I guess the trick will be to catch her in the office since she's so frequently out talking with people," said Beatrice.

Meadow said, "Oh, and we can maybe run by Trixie's on the way over? It's easier to park over there anyway and then just walk to the town hall."

"Don't tell me that *you've* got a chipped nail now! Not after giving me all that grief over mine," said Beatrice. She unconsciously picked up her pace again, Noo-noo trotting happily along beside her.

Meadow started huffing and puffing again. "Of course I haven't! Manicures cost too much for me to chip my polish immediately. No, I want to return that shampoo that she foisted on me. It smells wretched, and it made my hair greasy. I mean, kudos to Trixie for being such a good salesperson, but that stuff was no good."

Beatrice, realizing she'd sped up, slowed back down again. "Got it. Anything else on the agenda for tomorrow?"

"If we're lucky, maybe we can see Gene while we're at Goldie's. I still think his behavior on Monday when Devlin died was really weird. He could use a few follow-up questions."

Meadow stopped short. "Okay, that's enough exercise for me. I'm heading back to the car. You and Noo-noo enjoy the rest of your walk. And be sure to listen out for killers sneaking up behind you! Don't get all caught up in your thoughts again."

"Tomorrow at nine okay, then, for meeting at the salon? Then we can head right over to Goldie's. If we're going to have a shot at catching her, we should probably try early," said Beatrice.

Meadow was intent on getting back down the mountain toward her car and nodded without even turning around. "See you then!"

As she left, Beatrice heard Meadow's van make that really high-pitched whine and shook her head. Ramsay needed to listen to that and Meadow apparently kept forgetting or else it wasn't making that noise when she *did* try to show Ramsay. She'd have to remember to text Meadow when she got home to remind her about it.

The next morning, Beatrice woke up to the smell of breakfast food. She padded out to the kitchen to see a full pot of coffee, sunny-side up eggs and toast, and maple-flavored chicken sausage that Wyatt knew Beatrice especially liked.

She grinned at him. "Can we do this every morning?"

Wyatt laughed. "We could if you didn't usually wake up before I did. I was just glad to see that you were able to sleep in. You've been so busy that I figured you needed your sleep. Maybe your long walk with Noo-noo helped you to relax last night."

They sat down together and started eating. Beatrice said, "I did sort of sleep in, but I actually have plans this morning, so I should get ready just as soon as we're done." She took a big sip of coffee and then added a little more sugar to it. She could use the extra energy.

Wyatt nodded. "You and Meadow are heading over to see Goldie?"

"That's right. Meadow is obsessed with the fact that Goldie can't remember who told her about the sword. Although I still give her a pass for forgetting, considering all the people she talks to in a day." She took a bite of the sausage.

Wyatt said slowly, "And I definitely agree. Goldie talks to so many people that it would be easy to get confused. And maybe she doesn't want to come out and *say* who told her the information unless she was absolutely sure. After all, she knows that would incriminate the person."

"Right. She'd be throwing someone under the bus." Beatrice finished off her sausage and moved on to her sunny side-up eggs.

Wyatt said, "But she does have an *excellent* memory. I have worked with Goldie in the past on collaborative projects between the church and the town and have always been amazed that she is able to discuss the most minute details and costs without any sort of notes. Not only that, but she's a whiz at remembering people's names. I don't know how she does it. It's not just that she seems to know everybody in Dappled Hills, it's that she even remembers connections between them and where they used to work and where they work now. It's really phenomenal."

Beatrice was quiet for a few moments as she finished her food and thought about what Wyatt was telling her. "That's good to know, thanks. Definitely something to keep in mind. I was thinking that her memory was more like mine—just your average, everyday memory. I have a tough time remembering all the members of the church and I've been introduced to some of them multiple times."

"Yes, but you haven't always lived here. That gives Goldie more of an edge." He gave her a serious look. "You'll be careful, won't you? I don't want anything to happen to you. Call me if you run into any problems? I'm not doing anything today that I can't immediately leave."

"Of course I will," said Beatrice, reaching out to give him a quick kiss. "After all, I'm on the buddy system—I'm with Meadow all day. What could go wrong?"

"Let's not answer that question," said Wyatt with a crooked smile.

"And what about you? What's on your agenda for today? What exactly are you doing that you can so easily leave?"

"Meetings," said Wyatt ruefully. "I'd like to say that there was something else *besides* meetings, but that's all I have besides checking in with youth group tonight. Maybe the meetings will turn out more interesting than I think."

"Maybe," said Beatrice, with a smile. But did meetings ever turn out better? Wyatt always liked to look on the bright side.

Thirty minutes later, Beatrice pulled up in front of Trixie's salon. She saw no sign yet of Meadow and frowned, checking her watch. As she'd suspected, Beatrice herself was seven minutes late. She waited a few more minutes in the car, but even with the windows down, it was steamy on such a humid day.

Beatrice got out of the car and walked into the salon. She'd wait inside and Meadow could be as late as she liked. Although it was unusual for Meadow to run late at all. As scatterbrained as Meadow could seem, she ordinarily was fairly punctual. Maybe she'd forgotten that she'd wanted to return the shampoo before they talked to Goldie. She certainly had been laser-focused on Goldie, so that could be possible.

Trixie raised her head as the bell on the door rang. It looked as if she was the only one on duty that morning. She gave Beatrice a grin. "Another chip?"

Beatrice returned the grin, studying her nails. "That's a good guess, but it appears that I've been more careful. They're in pretty good shape. No, Meadow had an errand here, but she seems to be running late."

"You two still doing your sleuthing?" asked Trixie offhandedly.

Beatrice figured that Trixie, as owner of one of only a couple of salons in town, probably heard a ton of gossip each day. What was more, she probably *sought out* gossip. She likely became so used to hearing people's stories that she got hooked on it. The last thing she needed, though, was for Trixie to spread gossip about the investigation around town. Although Beatrice wouldn't mind *getting* some information from her.

"Oh, you know. Nothing official. We're just trying to make heads or tails of things," said Beatrice with a shrug. "Have you heard anything around town, though?"

Trixie gave her bark of a laugh. "Oh, I hear things. They may not be important things, but I hear them." She paused. "I did hear that Arnold Tremont, despite treating everyone to a big meal yesterday, is planning on leaving town for good."

"I think that's probably the case," said Beatrice nodding. People would realize that soon enough anyway when a real estate agent puts a sign up on the property. "He's always preferred living in a city. He might enjoy having a short vacation out here once a year, but I doubt he'd want to have a house to upkeep here."

Trixie sighed. "It's really just too bad. I hate the fact that that big house is going to sit empty like that."

"Maybe someone will snatch it up," said Beatrice.

Trixie shook her head. "It isn't likely though, is it? I sure can't see anybody in Dappled Hills buying it. No one would be able to afford it! I thought the same thing when it was being built. Wondered over the resale. Now it's going to have to be listed far and wide so that some rich person from a city somewhere will buy it as a vacation home."

Beatrice said, "You're right, it'll probably eventually go to someone from out of town. Dappled Hills is a beautiful location, and it seems like it's getting the attention from people as a retirement spot and vacation place."

Trixie was still thinking about the house itself. "I hope Arnold Tremont is getting all that stuff out of there. I don't think all that art junk adds to the house at all. If anything, it would distract from the house itself. People would be looking at all the tacky art and not the views from the windows and stuff. That house would show better to folks if it was empty."

Chapter Fifteen

Beatrice felt a small shiver go up her spine. She gave a half step back. "How did you know about the art? I thought you said that you'd never gone into the house."

Trixie gave a sharp laugh. "Right. No, I meant that I *figured* she had awful taste in art. I didn't even like some of her clothes. She had that avant-garde thing going on and I really just like normal, traditional stuff. Why not just wear tee-shirts and blue jeans if you're not doing anything special, right?"

Beatrice took a deep breath. "I hear you. It's just a little discrepancy, isn't it? Sort of like the discrepancy when you told me that you were working Monday evening when Devlin was killed."

Trixie put her manicured hands on her hips and gave Beatrice a belligerent stare. "What are you gabbing about? I *was* working that night."

"So you say. But a good friend of mine came by here to get a much-needed manicure and you weren't here. The other woman was here working by herself and she was booked up," said Beatrice.

Trixie narrowed her eyes. "Maybe I stepped out back for a cigarette. I was here."

Beatrice took another step behind her to the door. She could just bolt right out and call for help right now and half of downtown would be right there. But Trixie wasn't looking at all threatening. She was simply looking put-out.

"But there was someone else I know who I believe *did* get a manicure from you recently. Goldie Parsons," said Beatrice.

"Sure. Goldie came in here recently. Is that a crime? What of it?" asked Trixie suspiciously.

Beatrice glanced out the front window to see if she could see the Cavalry, in the unlikely form of Meadow Downey. But there was still no sign of Meadow. She cleared her throat and continued, "You see, Goldie and I had an interesting conversation at Annabelle's funeral service yesterday morning. She said that she'd heard that Annabelle had been killed with a sword."

Trixie shrugged.

"And you see, that's not the murder method that would be easily *guessed*. Who usually kills anyone with a sword? No one in this millennium. Someone must have given her the information about the sword," said Beatrice.

Trixie gave that short laugh again. "Are you just figuring out that this town is chock-full of gossips? It sure has taken you a while to reach that conclusion. And here I was thinking you were so smart."

"The problem with the gossip theory is that the police were careful not to disclose anything regarding the sword. Those of us who *did* know about it were cautioned by the police not to say anything about it. So that leaves the murderer as the only person who would know about the sword," said Beatrice. She continued listening out for the high-pitched whine of the van, but heard nothing other than the sound of her own heart pounding hard in her chest.

Trixie was quiet for a moment. "Then it sounds like Goldie Parsons is the murderer. Who'd have thought it? She always seemed like a goodie-goodie to me, but I guess that just goes to show that you can never really know somebody."

"No, what it actually says is that *you* are the murderer," said Beatrice solemnly. She edged again to position herself so that she could run through the front door of the shop.

Trixie went from being completely silent to giving a furious yell. She grabbed a pair of scissors and lunged at Beatrice. Trixie missed as Beatrice dodged her.

"Can't mind your own business!" shrieked Trixie as she raised her arm to try again.

At this moment, Meadow burst through the shop door. She took in the entire scene in one split second: Beatrice dodging the scissors, Trixie viciously trying to embed them in her. She heaved the bottle of shampoo she was returning at Trixie, which somehow made its mark, and then ran out the door again. "Ramsay!" she bellowed. "Help!"

Beatrice used the moment Trixie had been hit by the bottle to divest her of the scissors. Trixie, panting, backed away from her with a wild look in her eyes.

"It's over, Trixie," said Beatrice.

Trixie shook her head, still in denial, and turned to run to the back of the shop. Beatrice shoved her in the back as hard as she could, knocking her to the floor as Meadow approached them again, shaking with anger, and plopped down on top of Trixie's back to make sure she didn't move.

"And to think that I considered trying to recruit you into quilting! I thought your handiwork with your scissors would translate well into crafts. But you're not *worthy* of quilting," snarled Meadow as Ramsay ran through the door of the salon.

A few minutes later, with the state police called and on the way, and a handcuffed Trixie nearby, Ramsay said, "Now let's all go over this again. Exactly why did you go after Beatrice with a pair of scissors, Trixie? It sure doesn't sound like the typical way I'd imagine a store owner would greet a customer."

Trixie spat out, "She's no customer. She's just nosy."

Ramsay glanced at Beatrice's nails. "She sure has some nice nails for somebody who isn't a customer."

Trixie said, "She *has been* a customer. But today she was just poking around and making trouble."

Ramsay nodded slowly. "Okay then, I guess we'll start with Beatrice. She's likely to have more information for me this morning. Go ahead, Beatrice."

Beatrice took a deep breath. "Well, first off, I think that Trixie hasn't been totally honest. When she realized her husband, Elias, was having an affair with Annabelle, she didn't handle it with the equanimity that she was telling us about."

"In *English*," said Trixie in a bored voice.

"You were upset that Elias was having an affair. Very upset. I'm sure that you did give him that ultimatum that you mentioned, only because he did stop the affair. But I don't think, with my past experience of Annabelle, that she would have just blithely accepted the end of the relationship. It's much more likely that she would try to get Elias back and then dump *him* later. She was the type of person who liked things done on her own terms," said Beatrice.

Ramsay said, "So you mean she would have showed up at his house or something?"

Meadow just shook her head in disbelief at the very idea of these antics.

"I don't know if she'd do something like that. Far more likely that she called his phone or texted him a million times a day. Or flirted with him when she saw him at the grocery store or the pharmacy or somewhere," said Beatrice. "But there would have been contact, and not on Elias's side."

Trixie gave a short laugh. "Elias was terrified of the whole situation."

Beatrice nodded. "I'm sure he was. He had his wife threatening to leave him if he continued a relationship, and a woman who was determined to make sure the affair continued." She paused. "Clearly, you didn't mean to kill Annabelle . . . at least not at first. If you had, you'd have brought a weapon in with you."

Meadow said with a snort, "Like a pair of scissors."

"Well, scissors are her tools of the trade. She's probably very good with them," said Ramsay.

Trixie was sullenly silent.

Beatrice continued, "You'd have gone over there to have it out with her, though. To let her know to cut off all contact with Elias. But somehow the plan changed, didn't it? Maybe she laughed at you. Maybe she was condescending. Maybe she lifted up her phone and said she'd text him just as soon as you were out of there."

Trixie looked at her for a moment. "She didn't listen to me."

Beatrice said, "That sounds likely. Because, from what I know of Annabelle Tremont, she was not the sort of person to be dissuaded from anything that she wanted to do. And, if she wanted somehow to coerce your husband to continue their affair, that's exactly what she was going to do . . . and nothing you said would be able to stop her."

Ramsay said, "Annabelle must have felt safe with you, though, Trixie. She clearly turned her back on you for you to be able to get the sword off the wall and stab her with it."

Trixie shrugged. "Safe? I don't know. She just didn't see me as much of a threat."

"Well, that was very shortsighted of her!" said Meadow.

Trixie said, "She got a phone call. I don't think it was from Elias but she wanted me to think it was. She got all lovey-dovey and was cooing on the phone and stuff. I was so mad that I couldn't even see straight. I took down the sword and struck her down with it."

Beatrice gave a little shiver at the coldness of Trixie's voice. "You were quick-thinking. Even though you'd acted impulsively, you thought to wipe down the sword to make sure that there were no fingerprints. Then you left. You were probably careful when you left, too, making sure that no one saw you leave. The driveway was partially concealed by bushes and trees and would have possibly protected your car from being observed from the street."

Ramsay broke in. "But then Trixie *was* seen. Right? Maybe when she was leaving." He turned to Trixie. "You didn't know that Devlin Wilson was across the street showing a house to a client."

Trixie said laconically, "Typical. My bad luck."

Beatrice said, "What I don't know is whether you *saw* him see you, or whether he contacted you later to say that he'd seen you."

Trixie said, "What does it even matter? He saw me, all right. That's the only thing that mattered."

Beatrice said, "The thing is, Devlin was obsessed with Annabelle. She'd ended their relationship, but he'd have done anything to date her again. He was devastated to hear of her death. Maybe at first, he either didn't realize what he'd seen or wasn't exactly sure *who* he'd seen. Maybe he could tell it was a woman, but he couldn't see your face clearly. Maybe he only got a faint impression of your car. After all, it wouldn't have mattered at the time and he likely wouldn't have made any kind of mental note of it. It would only be later when he'd have figured that he must have seen Annabelle's murderer. And later that he realized it was you."

Trixie said, "Like I said, bad luck. I saw him as I was going into the salon. He was leaving the wine shop looking dejected. I could tell when he saw me that some lightbulb was going off."

"So you had to get rid of him," said Beatrice. "You left the shop and hurried over to Devlin's house. He was busy in his yard, working. He had his earbuds in and his music on and didn't hear you slip up behind him and quickly whack him on the head. And, miracle of miracles, no one seemed to see you this time, despite how public your crime was."

"Brazen!" said Meadow.

"Desperate," said Ramsay.

"Then you left and went back to the shop to finish up the evening there as if nothing had happened," said Beatrice. "But my friend noticed that you weren't there. She's been having a hard time lately and Meadow and I sent her over to your salon for a manicure as a treat. But, despite the alibi you gave, you weren't there to give her the manicure."

Trixie just sat there looking hostile.

Beatrice continued, "Goldie *was* able to get a manicure from you, however. And y'all apparently had a lot to talk about. I'm not sure what Goldie's contribution to the conversation was, but you at some point told her in an offhand way that Annabelle's murder weapon was a sword. That was privileged information that only the murderer would know. You'd also told me that you'd never set foot in the Tremont house. And yet you commented on their tacky art."

"Mistakes happen," said Trixie with a shrug of a shoulder.

"And all to save your marriage," said Meadow, still looking horrified.

Ramsay said, "Nope. Not to save her marriage. Her marriage with Elias would have worked out just fine. He'd decided to give up his affair with Annabelle and stick with Trixie. And when Elias sets his mind to something, he follows through. Annabelle's efforts to win him back would have come to nothing. If you'd wanted to do something, Trixie, you should have just gotten Elias into the station to file a complaint about harassment against Annabelle. That would have fixed her little red wagon."

"Exactly," said Beatrice. "Trixie wasn't saving her marriage by killing Annabelle. She was enacting revenge or acting out of fury or a combination of both."

"Well, Trixie, now we have to see how your marriage survives a bout of separation," said Ramsay with a sigh before he read Trixie her rights.

Meadow said to Beatrice, "Let's get out of here. Now this place is giving me the creeps."

"Where to?" asked Beatrice, just as eager to leave.

"Someplace close," said Ramsay, "In case we need you to give the state police a statement."

Meadow said, "Let's get over to June Bug's bakery then."

Beatrice nodded. "Let me just call Wyatt really quickly and fill him in on what happened."

Meadow said, "I'll meet you there . . . I'll just walk."

Wyatt picked right up. "Beatrice?"

Beatrice took a deep breath, which sounded a little shaky to her own ears. "Aren't you in the middle of a meeting?"

"Just finished one and the next one is rescheduled. What's up?" His voice was a little sharp with worry, knowing that Beatrice wouldn't have called him unless it was important.

Beatrice gave him as brief and as matter-of-fact of an update as she could.

"Where are you now?" he asked.

"I'm heading over to June Bug's with Meadow," said Beatrice.

"I'll meet you over there," he said quickly.

Beatrice arrived at the bakery to find an indignant Meadow filling June Bug in on Trixie's arrest. Beatrice also noticed a friendly woman at the cash register filling orders and checking customers out who must be June Bug's new help.

Savannah was on her way out of the door as Beatrice came in, a large bag in her hand. "Wish I could talk, but I'm heading over to Arrington Place," she said with a grin.

"Again? I know you volunteered there yesterday," said Beatrice.

"And organized a last-minute Scrabble tournament for today," said Savannah, looking pleased. "Thought I'd bring some snacks along. See you later!"

A few minutes later, Wyatt arrived at the bakery, giving Beatrice a long hug when he saw her. "I'm so glad you're okay," he murmured. Beatrice felt the remaining stress melt away in his arms.

Meadow said, "Know what else will make us feel better? Sugar! Pastries, anyone?"

They laughed, as Meadow had clearly hoped they would. And the pastries *did* look fantastic. June Bug had cinnamon-pecan buns, raspberry-swirl sweet rolls, and glazed lemon scones, for starters.

The three of them sat contentedly for a few minutes, eating their pastries and sipping their coffee. Then Wyatt said, "I'm still a little confused. Wasn't Meadow going to join you at the salon? Why were you there alone with Trixie? And, actually, why were you at the salon at all? I'd thought you were going to speak with Goldie."

Meadow nodded ruefully. "That was the original plan. We were only running by the salon for a minute to return a bottle of shampoo I'd bought there." She brightened. "But I guess I *did* make it there, only a bit late."

"You came in like an action hero," said Beatrice with a laugh. "Flinging that bottle of shampoo with deadly precision."

"Well, it made me mad! That Trixie with her scissors," fumed Meadow. "I can't imagine what got into her."

Beatrice gave a shiver thinking about the scissors and then said to Wyatt, "I'm going to make a deduction, since I'm still in sleuthing mode. I think that Meadow *would* have been there on time if the van hadn't broken down. Meadow is ordinarily very prompt everywhere we go. But her van has been making funny noises for the last week."

Meadow grimaced. "You were right about that. I shouldn't have ignored what the van was trying to tell me. But it simply wouldn't make that noise when I tried to show it to Ramsay."

"Your van wouldn't start this morning?" asked Wyatt.

"It would turn over, but it wouldn't go. We had to wait for the car to be towed and then I had to wait longer for Ramsay to finish up and give me a ride over to the salon. I should have texted Beatrice, but I was hoping it wasn't going to take that long," Meadow said.

Beatrice snorted. "Even if you'd texted me, I might not have been able to answer it, under the circumstances. Besides, it ended up working out well. I went inside to wait because it was so hot outside that I couldn't wait in the car. Then Trixie and I started talking, and she threw out that statement about 'tacky art,' which got me thinking about all the other clues. And when you finally did show up, you came in with guns blazing. So to speak."

Meadow finished chewing her sweet roll and said, "At least peace is restored in Dappled Hills again. And here we are eating breakfast together again, just like normal."

"Except that Ramsay isn't with us," said Wyatt.

Meadow waved her hand in the air. "Yes, but this part, getting Trixie booked and whatnot, won't take as long as investigating murders. He's at the tail-end of a case. He'll be back home later today, reading a book and sipping a glass of wine with Boris lying at his feet."

Beatrice and Wyatt looked at each other.

"Actually, that sounds like an amazing idea," said Beatrice slowly.

Wyatt said, "We could bring our own wine. And our own books."

"And your own corgi!" said Meadow. "It's a plan."

About the Author:

Elizabeth writes the Southern Quilting mysteries and Memphis Barbeque mysteries for Penguin Random House and the Myrtle Clover series for Midnight Ink and independently. She blogs at ElizabethSpannCraig.com/blog, named by Writer's Digest as one of the 101 Best Websites for Writers. Elizabeth makes her home in Matthews, North Carolina, with her husband. She's the mother of two.

Sign up for Elizabeth's free newsletter to stay updated on releases:

https://elizabethspanncraig.com/newsletter/

This and That

I love hearing from my readers. You can find me on Facebook as Elizabeth Spann Craig Author, on Twitter as elizabethscraig, on my website at elizabethspanncraig.com, and by email at elizabethspanncraig@gmail.com.

Thanks so much for reading my book...I appreciate it. If you enjoyed the story, would you please leave a short review on the site where you purchased it? Just a few words would be great. Not only do I feel encouraged reading them, but they also help other readers discover my books. Thank you!

Did you know my books are available in print and ebook formats? And most of the Myrtle Clover series is available in audio. Find them on Audible or ITunes.

Interested in having a character named after you? In a preview of my books before they're released? Or even just your name listed in the acknowledgments of a future book? Visit my Patreon page at https://www.patreon.com/elizabethspanncraig
.

I have Myrtle Clover tote bags, charms, magnets, and other goodies at my Café Press shop: https://www.cafepress.com/cozymystery

If you'd like an autographed book for yourself or a friend, please visit my Etsy page.

I'd also like to thank some folks who helped me put this book together. Thanks to my cover designer, Karri Klawiter, for her awesome covers. Thanks to my editor, Judy Beatty, for all of her help. Thanks to beta readers Amanda Arrieta and Dan Harris for all of their helpful suggestions and careful reading. Thanks, as always, to my family and readers.

Other Works by the Author:

Myrtle Clover Series in Order (be sure to look for the Myrtle series in audio, ebook, and print):

Pretty is as Pretty Dies

Progressive Dinner Deadly

A Dyeing Shame

A Body in the Backyard

Death at a Drop-In

A Body at Book Club

Death Pays a Visit

A Body at Bunco

Murder on Opening Night

Cruising for Murder

Cooking is Murder

A Body in the Trunk

Cleaning is Murder

Edit to Death (2019)

Southern Quilting Mysteries in Order:

Quilt or Innocence

Knot What it Seams

Quilt Trip

Shear Trouble
Tying the Knot
Patch of Trouble
Fall to Pieces
Rest in Pieces
On Pins and Needles
Fit to be Tied (2019)

The Village Library Mysteries in Order (Debuting 2019):
Checked Out (2019)

Memphis Barbeque Mysteries in Order (Written as Riley Adams):
Delicious and Suspicious
Finger Lickin' Dead
Hickory Smoked Homicide
Rubbed Out

And a standalone "cozy zombie" novel: Race to Refuge, written as Liz Craig

Printed in the USA
CPSIA information can be obtained
at www.ICGtesting.com
LVHW010924210724
786093LV00030B/782

9 781946 227324